o

The Comr

The Commune

§§

Oliver Black

Ashgrove Publishing
London

You are praising me for something which, in my opinion, has not been a very difficult achievement. A person who lacks the means, within himself, to live a good and happy life will find any period of his existence wearisome. But rely for life's blessings on your own resources, and you will not take a gloomy view of any of the inevitable consequences of nature's laws. Everyone hopes to attain an advanced age; yet when it comes they all complain! So foolish and perverse can people be.

Cicero, *De Senectute*

Chapter 1

•

There was a whirr of increasing volume and – more alarmingly – pitch, then a clank, a grunt (as of one winded), a half-second's silence, a thud, as a heavy object hit the floor, and a bump on my door, which sprang open. As a result, the cunning analysis of the concept of independent promises in English contract law, which was just edging into my mind, edged out of it again. Intellectual work demands silence, which I have hunted remorselessly and fruitlessly throughout my academic life. I tried earplugs, but they gave me tinnitus and for some reason left me hard of hearing after I took them out. Eventually I accepted that, if you're highly strung, you will find something to disturb you in a padded cell, and I have since tried, and failed, to live by the ancient dictum that serenity is achieved by adjusting your desires to your circumstances, rather than the other way round. But there are limits to the dictum's sensible application, and to have your door burst open while you are inserting the keystone into the arch of a lifetime's jurisprudential achievement is beyond them. *Conceptual Foundations of Contract*, as my book is provisionally called, should do for me what *Dad's Army* did for Arthur Lowe – console me in later life with the richly deserved rewards of fame and honour that eluded me in my prime. It will be a kick in the teeth for (a) the misguided and ungenerous bastards at a nameless Cambridge college who withheld the fellowship that would have adorned their institution and suited me so well and (b) the fuckers at my last university who denied me the professorship that would have improved by 18 per cent the pension on which, for the past 17 years, I have been surviving, impotently watching the gap increase between RPI and my spending power and the gentility drain from my poverty. I would now be turned away with a sneer by (if it still exists) the Distressed Gentlefolks' Aid Association, which used to place small advertisements at the bottom of the *Sunday Telegraph*'s front page, opposite RUKBA's 'We, the limbless, look to you for help'. (A one-legged ex-serviceman smiled bravely as he leant on the arm of a kind and rather attractive nurse.)

In dark moments I wonder whether intellectual achievement of a high order is possible at age 77. I choose to believe that jurists, unlike mathematicians, take many decades to ripen, but there is doubtless a point at which you start to forget things more quickly than you learn them. My concentration too is getting worse, which makes noise the more distracting. In short, I'm terrified of declining powers, let alone of going senile, the way poor Joy has gone since we all moved in here – a hideous and heartbreaking transition from astute sensitivity and common sense, to endearing vagueness, to irritating confusion, to what the Caring Professions call 'confusion', viz. shit-smearing gaga. Worst are the bouts of truculence, so incongruous in that once gentle lady. How Dennis copes, Christ knows: the day centre is a blessing. Generally I think I'm still alert enough for everyday use, but no doubt there are forms of dementia characterised by the fact that if you have them you don't think you have.

I felt obliged to go to the door to identify the person from Porlock. It was Howard, struggling to transform himself from shapeless heap to homo erectus and in the process encroaching further on my territory. His glasses had fallen off and his hearing-aid had shot an uncanny distance down the landing. Various items had tumbled from his overstuffed pockets, inter alia a half-smoked Hamlet and a sandwich, past its prime, containing – I speculate – tongue. As I approached, he was hurriedly reinserting his dentures. Never secure in his mouth, these once flew from it on to the dining-table when he sneezed, so he now wraps his lips around them when sneezing, coughing or – more bizarrely and less necessarily – laughing. He laughed (thus) bravely as I helped him to his feet.

'Ha ha ha. God Almighty, nearly propelled into an early grave there! Bloody Escalope's got a mind of its own. Psychotic, in fact. It did one of those surges just as we were reaching the landing.'

Segunda called the stairlift the 'Escalope' and now we all do. She is Spanish and, although she came to England five years ago, her English has failed to progress. The reasons are first that she's usually listening to music through earphones and second that she lives with an inarticulate lout. The general opinion is that she moved mentally from stairlift to escalator to Escalope. She used to be in catering – a part of her history hard to infer from the meals she cooks for us.

'The Escalope never surged before you "overhauled" it,' I replied. 'And the seat was low enough for all users to reach the footrest. Now the girls dangle their legs, which makes the surges all the more dangerous. Amelia nearly came off last week. You'd better pray that Joy stays off it.'

'Dennis says it's out of bounds for Joy.'

'Joy wouldn't know a bound from a leap. Also, you shouldn't have been using the Escalope. You don't need it. Your main problems are obesity, excessive and untreated perspiration, and self-abuse in the form of cigarettes and alcohol. The first would be alleviated by exercise – specifically by walking upstairs.'

Most people, when they reach our age, have long been losing body mass: the result is that the very old often look more like their young selves than they do their middle-aged selves. But Howard goes on getting fatter. His face is now so bloated that it looks as if he had stuffed his cheeks with newspaper – a Sunday one with all the supplements – or were storing food in them like a hamster. The fat has ironed out his wrinkles – the opposite way of looking young.

'I take exercise,' he replied. 'It worsens the second problem.'

He kicked off his decaying loafers – having lumbered, despite the Do Not Disturb sign, into my room and seated himself in my favourite chair – to display the degenerate state of his socks, one of which was worn to the threshold of non-existence toewards of the heel. All the toes of the foot in question were visible and four had nails of mandarin length, but the big one had, in place of a nail, a smooth dome of flesh. Before I could worry about the risk of odours from that quarter, he had rekindled the Hamlet: this I kept an eye on, remembering the visit of the fire brigade after Howard had stuck a still-smouldering cigar in the pocket of his coat, Segunda had tidied it away in the cupboard by the front door, and the whole cupboard had gone up. Two of Amelia's minks were incinerated.

He didn't stoop to defend himself further against my animadversions on his hobbies, fitness, hygiene and use of drugs. He clearly had something on his mind that he wanted, so to speak, to get off his chest.

'I just came up for a chat. Hope I'm not interrupting anything.'

'No no, I was sitting here hoping for a visit from you.'

He was too preoccupied to respond to irony. Generally he has a level of self-obsession suited more to a teenager than to a buffer crowding 80: any conversation he will wrench, if he can, round to his own concerns. This, combined with his swinish habits, may explain why he has got through four wives. Another possible explanation is that domestic turmoil compensated for the tedious regularity of his work: unworried about achievement, Howard drudged placidly in the middle ranks of the civil service for 40 years – Home Office, Trade, 'Ag and Fish' and, lastly, Transport, where he was infected with a tiresome and now chronic interest in trains. The wife he loved most was the first, Kath, whom he met when we were all students and who left him after two years. Things went downhill after he noticed, in a pub, that she was reading a beer-mat while he was sounding off about something. None of her successors, as Howard has often pointed out, came up to Kath's standards. The last one, Rosalind, despite being much younger than Howard and thus a good bet so far as concerned companionship and nursing in old age, died four years ago, which moved him to join us. The two middle wives (together with Howard) produced six children, who in turn have spawned uncountable grandchildren, and there is an extensive illegitimate brood – including a great-grand-child – resulting from a number of flings. The middle wives still dun him for alimony, making him – after me – the poorest person here.

It was a matter of the heart he wanted to talk about. 'What's your opinion on sex at our age?' he asked.

This was clearly the prologue to a discussion of some particular sexual concern of his. Still exasperated by the loss of the insight into independent promises, I wasn't minded to make things easy for him. 'There are two, but the differences become harder to discern,' I replied.

'I mean, I don't think we should be bound by stereo-types.'

I remained silent.

He circled in on his preoccupation. 'Take me, for instance. I'm in pretty good nick. My Johnson still stands up. And I'm pretty attractive to the fair sex.' (I can't abide that cliché; Schopenhauer was nearer the mark with his stunted, narrow-shouldered, broad-hipped and short-legged sex.) 'So what's wrong with a bit of a tumble, if she's willing?'

'Why are you asking me this? Ever since you moved in here you've pursued anything with two legs and a hole in a convenient place – with occasional success, judging from what I hear through the wall. In fact, I doubt you're too particular about the two legs. I'll say nothing about Rosalind's funeral baked meats.'

Obviously he had a specific woman in mind, but I wasn't

going to help him, so there was a pause. Finally he came out with, 'Segunda's a sweet girl.'

His eyes went small and piggish, as they do when he's drunk. In fact he may have had a few before coming up. The Hamlet prevented my telling from his breath, and nothing could be inferred from the time of day: one morning at breakfast he finished off two-thirds of a bottle of wine left on the sideboard from the previous night's dinner.

'You can, as that tennis twerp said, not be serious. In the first place, she has refused to enter your room since the toast-and-marmalade incident.' I was referring to the time when Segunda, while cleaning Howard's room, found two pieces of toast and Wilkin's Double One under the bedclothes – a limit case of breakfast in bed. It was the last straw for Segunda: the room is a bomb-site and, as Howard never opens the windows, the smell – old Hamlets, older clothes, decomposing food – is unbearable. I wonder whether Polanski ever knew him.

'She refused to *clean* my room.'

'So you think that, although she refuses to make your bed because it's got your breakfast in it, she might be prepared to lie on top of the breakfast and kick her little legs in the air while you prove to her that you can still get blood into your Johnson?'

'We wouldn't have to meet in my room.'

'Where do you suggest? Behind the hedge? In Oik's shed? And what do you suppose Oik will do when he finds you on the job? You'll get blood in a lot of other places.'

'Oik' is our witty transformation of 'Ike', the name by which Segunda's boyfriend is known to his friends. No-one seems to know the name on his birth certificate. He lives with Segunda in an outhouse: she can only have taken him in because it's hard to tell how horrible someone of another nationality is. Oik, a road-mender, is detectable by the smell of tar or, when it is in the ascendant, aftershave. He is stupid and aggressive, has a criminal record embracing drug abuse, antisocial behaviour and aggravated assault, and mistreats Segunda. Frequent obstacles to my concentration are their screaming rows and their equally noisy copulations. Often it's hard to tell whether you're hearing a fight or a bit of nooky: no doubt there are transitions in each direction. Some valuable items – silver knick-knacks, Roland's fountain pen, Barbara's iPad – have disappeared: everyone suspects Oik, but no-one dares say anything, for fear of offending, and thus losing, Segunda. Also, as none of us likes to admit, at our age you can't be sure you haven't just mislaid something.

'All things considered,' I concluded, 'you have an embarrassment of reasons to keep your Johnson away from Segunda. Why Johnson, anyway?'

The exchange was cut short by the gong for supper. At the top of the stairs, where the Escalope had tossed Howard, we passed a new manifestation of Barbara's authoritarian personality, a sign saying:

DOWNSTAIRS THIS WAY

'You may think it funny,' Barbara growled tartly in her baritone as she emerged from her room and found us deriding the sign, 'but it's hard for Joy to find her way around.'

'She never comes up here,' I replied. 'And where's it going to end? Name tags for the residents? Signs on the spoons saying "spoon"? Signs on the signs saying "sign"?' She pushed past without a further word and cantered downstairs.

Chapter 2

•

It was Bunny's turn to cook. Segunda doesn't do in the evenings, so there's a rota for the preparation of supper. This has led to various disputes, Dennis and Joy being the subjects of a recurring one. Joy is nominally on the rota, but was forbidden to cook by herself after she served, as a starter, Moth's cat food on some Ryvita. Barbara, Moth's doting owner, was incensed and commented, within earshot of both Joy and Dennis, about Joy's readiness for a home; but it was an easy mistake for anyone in full possession of her faculties to make, the cat food being some ridiculous 'gourmet' confection. The result is that Dennis helps Joy on her nights but also has nights allotted to him alone, so the dispute concerns double counting. Dennis hasn't complained, but Bunny and I have stood up for him against Barbara's assertion that he should take the rough with the smooth (it being unclear what the smooth is in this instance). So far Barbara has won, as she holds sway over Amelia, who writes the rota.

Other problems with the rota are that people 'forget' to cook, or to tell Segunda what to buy, or they prepare something uneatable. Howard's last contained kelp and sea-slugs. Consistently the worst cook is Roland, who had never boiled an egg till he came here. He makes a song and dance and uses all the utensils, only to produce a moronically simple dish such as the one he recently announced as 'Roland's Famous Chicken Salad' — an emetic sludge of skinless chicken breasts which he had put under the grill for a bot-ulism-guaranteeingly brief period, salad cream, tinned pineapple and Jolly Green Giant corn. Amelia refused to touch any, having seen from the packet how cheap the breasts were: she speculated that they had been 'grown by scientists'. People accordingly find reasons to go out on Roland's nights: there is an otherwise improbably keen interest in the offerings of the local adult education institute, Barbara having signed up for 'dance and movement' (the former presumably entails the latter) and Amelia for 'opera appreciation', which has given her a taste for archaic Italian ejaculations at moments of crisis. 'Ohimè' or 'Gran' dio' she cries if something goes wrong, and she once, more wittily, called 'Vai, barbara' as Barbara left the room. Her only other knowledge of Italian is 'Dove il gabinetto'.

Bunny is an able and conscientious chef, despite her emphysema (she persists in calling it 'envysemia'), which makes her constantly breathless: the Escalope is a necessity for her, and she starts to wheeze even as she climbs on to it – the climb in turn being a necessity since Howard mucked around with the seat. From a snapshot, however, you would judge her a paragon of vigorous old age: short, tubby-to-spherical and red-cheeked – a character from Beatrix Potter, down to the whiskers. She endures her rotten health with good cheer and, taking into account the emotional refrigerator that her marriage to Roland has been, the warmth of her heart is a caloric victory. It was hard at the time to see what brought them together: she, then pretty and ringletted, was ebullient and sociable and never fed her brain with anything richer than the occasional cookery book or women's magazine; he was gloomy, reclusive and intellectual – traits that he has since developed to the point of self-parody, especially the gloom.

'When I woke up from my nap this afternoon,' he said, hunched at the kitchen table and making no move towards helping Bunny, who was at work on a Spanish omelette, 'I decided I was already dead.'

His favourite saying is 'Everything is getting worse', which he calls Roland's Theorem. The gloom is leavened by wit but tinctured by pomposity: when Howard recently invited to Sunday lunch one Peggy, whom he had met at the Over-Sixties and seemed to fancy, Peggy politely asked Roland about his career.

'I'm a literary critic,' he drawled, 'or rather *was*, for I've been dead for years so far as the reading public is concerned.'

Peggy asked him what his last book had been about.

'Dostoyevsky's ontology of evil,' said Roland. 'I'm afraid you're unlikely to be interested or to understand. It's fairly abstract stuff.'

'I might have a faint inkling. I taught metaphysics and ethics at London University for many years.' There were some smirks among the convives.

Roland is now made additionally lugubrious by ill-health, which he bears less stoically than does Bunny. Formerly tall and gauntly handsome, he is starting to shrink and bend from osteoporosis, and has a touch of the circus clown in his now oversized clothes. He repeatedly predicts that soon he will be so bent that he'll have to find his way with a mirror. On top of that he has Parkinson's, which has largely wiped the play of expression from his face. The disease is controlled by a cocktail of drugs that produce distressing side-effects. As it progresses, the consultant varies the cocktail by trial and error, and during the error phase Roland gets fits of the shakes, which embarrass and enrage him, the more so because they make him dependent on Bunny, who in his eyes is now no more than an irritant who can say or do nothing right.

One result of Roland's neglect of and contempt for Bunny, and his dismissive refusal to supply her with the children she would have raised so happily and well, is that her affection has been deflected to a series of pets. A dumb animal can't absorb with dignity the love that Bunny has to offer: the present incumbent – a yapping abortion called Jeeves ('Jif' in Segunda's rendering) – has been ruined by it. Another result is that the rest of us feel sorry for Bunny and therefore indulge her wittering: we often hear more than we might want about her trivial purchases of yore, with precise but unverifiable details of place, time and cost.

'Do you know, I've had this apron since 1962,' she said as she staggered to the table with the first pan of omelette. 'I bought it for 15 shillings at Peter Jones. There was another one, in red, which looked smarter, but I thought the stains wouldn't show so much on the green.'

Glazed smiles were exchanged. The apron bore a full-sized picture of the naked Venus, the picture including all but the head, lower legs and feet, so that Venus appeared to have Bunny's.

'That pheasant was on the bird-table again this afternoon, making it sway about,' Bunny continued seamlessly. 'Did you see him, darling?' (this to Joy). 'It's worn very well, much better than that stripy thing I got at the market in – where was that lovely market in the Dordogne, Roland? – for 60 francs.'

'In the Dordogne,' mumbled Roland, who had taken up the *London Review of Books*. As he leant over the table, his head appeared to be growing out of his chest.

'Dennis is late,' said Joy impatiently. 'Where are the children?'

Joy looks as slender and graceful, in her Pre-Raphaelite way, as she did at age 20 – an instance of a very old self resembling a young self. Mentally, Joy now resembles her very young self. Two of her children, who have children of their own, are in London. The third lives in Argentina. None was expected here for supper. Joy made to get up from the table, but was restrained by Barbara.

Bunny said, 'So lucky we had all those *eggs* with their funny Bs.'

'What!' cried Barbara. 'Where did you find those eggs?'

Sighs ensued as we realised we were in for another boundary dispute about the fridge. Each couple and singleton has been allotted its/his/her own shelf in the giant SMEG (Amelia can't understand why Howard and Bernard find this name entertaining), but the convention is continually breached: food moves without the owner's consent from one shelf to another, or into someone else's mouth or, because it has gone rotten and is spreading disease and stink, into the dustbin. Usually the person who has thrown it away won't own up, despite having performed a public service, and the incident is blamed on Segunda behind her back.

'Those eggs were on my shelf. B is for Barbara. You've flagrantly flaunted the rules.' When she is angry her voice goes even deeper than usual.

'Flagrantly flouted,' murmured Roland without looking up from the LRB.

Bunny smiled pluckily. 'I thought it was B for Bunny.'

'Don't be such a damn fool.' Barbara can be breathtakingly rude.

A silence fell. Bunny started what she calls 'plating up'.

'Giusti numi, how divine. An ormlit!' gushed Amelia when she received her helping. She preserves an accent last current in the age of *Brief Encounter*: 'about' she pronounces 'a bite', 'hot' becomes 'hut', and 'yes', 'ears'. The accent is so strong that we all suspect it to have been cultivated to cover one that would betray humble origins. (Sometimes, indeed, she utters a cockneyism, but that may have been the effect of a nanny.) Her claim to be descended from the Habsburgs is supported by a bulldozer chin, but none of us is convinced, so Roland christened her the Perhapsburg.

'Dennis is *late*,' Joy repeated, more petulantly. She often says this, irrespective of the circumstances and quite often when Dennis is sitting beside her, but on this occasion her statement was true if unjustified.

'If Dennis doesn't make himself available to look after Joy, she won't be able to stay here,' said Barbara. 'It's not fair on the rest of us.'

Joy glanced at her sharply. Barbara went to bang the gong again: having a head of steam to let off because of the eggs, she bashed the thing so hard, it almost fell from its hooks.

'Fire!' cried Joy, smiling serenely.

'A job for you at the Rank Organisation,' said Bernard as Barbara came back into the kitchen.

I volunteered to go and look for Dennis, despite the congealing effect this would have on my piece of ormlit. I found him in what is known as the gym – less grandiosely, a dark shed containing a few second-hand fitness machines, themselves unfit and a danger to health. Despite the sign that Barbara has stuck inside the door – THINK OF OTHERS AND WIPE SWEAT FROM MACHINES AFTER USE – I occasionally take a turn myself on the cycling machine, keeping my will power up by pretending that the flywheel generates an electric current that passes through wires to the testicles or tits (depending) of someone I hate, whose hair in consequence stands on end: the harder I pedal, the more excruciating the shock endured by the imagined victim (most recently my former head of department, author of an absurdly well received monograph on tortious remedies). Dennis, having been advised by our GP, Dr Pee, to alleviate arthritis in the hip by cycling, is usually found in the gym at seven in the evening, when he can catch up with *The Archers* (there's a Brixton Briefcase there for the purpose). Sometimes he takes Joy along and lets her have a go on the cycle: as she pedals, she appears to think she is going somewhere.

Dennis was prone on the floor with one foot caught by the strap of the cycling machine's pedal. The Archers were long past and Radio 4 was on to *Moral Maze*, that nauseating farrago of pompous ranting that holds itself out as perceptive debate. I switched it off before turning to Dennis.

'Thank God you've come, dear boy,' he said as heartily

as he could manage. 'I lost my balance getting off. I've been stuck in this balletic position for over an hour. I gave up calling. I'm lucky not to have broken something.'

Contrary to the purpose of the cycling, his hip had seized up during the 70 minutes Dennis had lain on the cold lino, and he was practically hopping as we crossed the yard. He was shivering too, in his T-shirt and shorts. I suggested that we go straight into the kitchen to salvage the supper, but he insisted on, as he self-deludingly put it, running upstairs to wash and change: a stickler, he always wears jacket and tie for dinner, which endears him to Amelia as much as Howard disdears himself to her by turning up dressed as a vagrant. Amelia says that you can judge a man by his shoes, so her judgment of Dennis is favourable: his Lobb brogues, which he polishes on the kitchen table every night, have that precious and elusive glow that causes the phrase 'orrible little man' to die on the lips of sergeant-majors.

When Dennis reappeared, he was wearing a blazer and his face was red and shiny, as if polished like his shoes.

'Where's Dennis?' Joy snapped at him as he came in.

He gave her a kiss. The others had moved on to a treacle pudding that Bunny had made from scratch — a waste of effort in my view, as the microwaveable ones from M&S are just as good — and I was trying to catch up by gobbling my omelette segment, which had become cold and rubbery. Dennis's was rigid, like a floor tile.

'Not at all bad, Bunny dear,' he said. 'And strengthens the jaws.'

Chapter 3

•

We all know that there's little to be said for old age – apart from the old and doubtful saw that it's better than the alternative – and that the things against it are mostly losses: of status, faculties, health, hopes and friends. It had long seemed to me that something could be done as to the last by binding a group of elderly chums together in a commune. Three years ago I therefore suggested to my old friends Bernard and Amelia Bankes that I move into their house with a group of our cronies to provide good cheer and solace to each other as the twilight thickened. The suggestion was less impertinent than it might seem, for the house – which is mysteriously called The Graylings and is located near Ongar in subrural Essex – is a pile. Bernard was, as his surname suggests, a banker and had to do something with his vast income, but The Graylings had been far too big for the Bankeses even when their daughter Sarah was growing up; Sarah had left home decades previously, and Bernard and Amelia rattled around the house like the Kanes in Xanadu. They liked my idea and there were several candidates. It suited me: I was living at the time, in increasingly straitened circs, in a rented ground-floor flat on an arterial road. Rosalind had just died, leaving Howard at sea. Bunny jumped at the proposal, for the unrelieved company of Roland was worse than solitude, and they also needed to release the equity in their house. More surprising was the enthusiasm of Dennis and Joy, who lived comfortably in a large house in Kew and had another one in Provence, but they were feeling stale and depressed and were probably frightened by Joy's increasing forgetfulness. Dennis sold the two houses and bought a flat in the Barbican for trips to London, which decreased in frequency as Joy increased in senility and have now ceased.

And so we all moved into The Graylings – a house as ugly as it is big, built during the teens of the last century in a style found, as Roland put it, more in Harrow than in Ongar, with mock-Tudor gables and a tangle of exterior piping: fittingly, it looks like an old folks' home. The couples inhabit the piano nobile, the singletons – Howard, Barbara and I – the second floor. Barbara is, as Dennis embarrassingly said, the nigger in the woodpile: whereas the rest of us have been buddies for over half a century, Barbara is by our standards a recent accretion and is a friend of Amelia alone. Barbara was a career woman in the days before that was a respected role, running a reasonably successful textile business, where she developed her taste for bossing people around. So far as I know, she never married. Having somehow inserted herself into The Graylings a couple of years before the commune was instituted, she clearly resents our incursion, as she seems to crave a secluded intimacy with Amelia (Barbara has always ignored Bernard and he is happy to return the favour). Perhaps there's a sexual undercurrent, but once you start looking for those you find them everywhere: you might as easily attribute to Dennis designs on Oik, on the basis of the strange taste he has for Oik's company. I recently witnessed a long, if one-sided, conversation between them in the yard, Dennis lolling benignly against the gate and burbling while Oik stuck blood-curdling transfers to the tank of his motorbike. Come to think of it, there has always been something a bit fey about Dennis.

Chapter 4

•

Quite a day. Before breakfast I stepped on to the terrace for a breath of air. It was a delightful crisp and dewy autumn morning, the sounds of nature, and of the main road, broken occasionally by cracks from Bernard's shotgun: some of our dumb friends were, like Miss Otis, not going to make it to lunch. Bernard likes to take pot-shots at anything winged or four-legged that happens to be in The Graylings' garden at dawn or dusk. One shot was at something unwinged and two-legged, namely the gardener Mr Shanks ('Mr' is archaic these days, but not even Amelia has any idea what his first name is), who took a lot of placating after a near miss. Bernard claimed to have mistaken him for a badger.

I thought of waiting for Bernard to emerge from the bushes before I went in, for he is usually prompt at the trough; but my appetite was lusty, so I carried on without him. Also it was risky hanging around when he was at large with his gun: I too might be mistaken for a badger. By the time we had finished breakfast Bernard had still not appeared, despite the fact that the cracking of the gun had long ceased, so we dispersed, leaving his bacon to rigidify and his scrambled eggs to gelatinise on the hot plate. I went upstairs to write and was an hour into the vexed question whether an agreement can be analysed into undertakings by the parties when I was distracted by a frenzied banging of the gong. It is never sounded for elevenses, and in any case it wasn't yet eleven, so the communards emerged from their lairs to see what was up. The banger was Bunny, whose face was unusually red even by its own high standards. She was panting more than usual and her mouth was ajar. When we were quorate she stopped banging and announced, 'I've found Bernard. I went to the herb garden for some sage. I always think it's better than thyme for stuffing, even when you're doing chicken.'

Clearly she was starting a frolic of free association, so Dennis intervened. 'You've found Bernard,' he said firmly.

'Yes.' She looked round at us with a bright, tense smile.

'And?'

Bunny continued smiling inanely. Some of us cast nervous glances at Amelia, who was serene and majestic as usual.

Dennis pressed on. 'Has something happened to Bernard?'

'He's dead,' Bunny said in a small voice.

Barbara moved to Amelia's side. More looks of concern were directed at Amelia, but her manner was unchanged: a patrician smile played above her bulldozer chin. You can never be sure whether she has heard.

Bunny continued in the same little voice, 'He's dead, in the herb garden. He's squashing the rosemary.'

We hovered in bewilderment till Barbara stepped in. 'Don't just stand there like mushrooms,' she barked. 'He might be still alive.' She had already pulled on her flat cap and was striding towards the back door. The rest of us followed, like schoolchildren trotting after teacher.

Bunny's description of the scene in the herb garden was accurate so far as it went. Bernard was lying on his back, his top half sprawled over the bed, squashing not only the rosemary but the parsley and what the slugs and rabbits had spared of the sorrel. One rabbit had paid the price: a victim of Bernard's erratic aim, it lay bloody and twitching near a lavender bush. Bernard's pale blue eyes were wide open, so it was pretty clear that he was dead. The gun lay beside him with its barrel pointing at his head, but there was no sign of a wound: it looked like a heart attack – one of those that people insist on calling 'massive'.

'Are we sure he's dead?' said Amelia with unshaken gentility. She could have been making small-talk at a cocktail party.

Howard bent over and bellowed 'BERNARD!' in Bernard's ear.

'Don't be so bloody ridiculous, Howard,' said Barbara. 'Get out of the way. Let me feel his pulse: I'm a first-aider.' She would be. She felt Bernard's wrist, then pressed her ear to his chest, then placed the palm of her hand near his open mouth, then the back of her hand on his cheek. 'It's cold already,' she said. 'He's dead – there's no doubt about it. We'll have to call an ambulance.'

'What's the point, if he's dead?' said Roland, unable to resist smart-aleckery even in an emergency.

'Before anything else happens,' said Amelia, 'I'd be grateful if you'd all join me in the drawing-room.' She sounded like a duchess magnanimously summoning her staff to attend the presentation of a gold watch to an old retainer.

'We can't leave him lying there,' Barbara protested.

Roland: 'He won't run away.'

'*Please*, Roland,' said Dennis.

We gathered in the drawing-room and settled into our favourite chairs and bits of sofa. Amelia, however, remained standing, her self-possession intact. Perhaps the shock had not yet sunk in, or perhaps she had read her Seneca, or perhaps she hated Bernard and was glad that he was dead. Even so, you'd think a person would be shaken when her spouse of more than 50 years suddenly keels over.

'I'm afraid,' she declared, 'that Bernard's death puts me – well, all of us – in rather a difficult position. You see, The Graylings won't come to me: I've got large debts – a left-over from the Lloyds thing – so Bernard's will leaves everything to Sarah.'

Sarah is the only fruit of Amelia and Bernard. She lives in America with her dismal Scottish husband Angus: I have met them only twice, when they came on their brief annual visits.

'But Sarah will surely allow things to continue as they are?' said Bunny. 'She's hardly going to put her dear old mum on the street.'

Amelia smiled sourly. 'Dear old mum isn't quite the phrase, I'm afraid. Sarah and I have never got on. In fact, that's putting it mildly. She'll see my desire to stay here as a reason for pushing me out. As for the rest of you –'

'I doubt she could do that,' said Dennis. 'It's not my patch, Amelia, but there are occupiers' rights and that sort of thing.'

'She could have a jolly good try: you know what she's like.' Amelia paused. 'She's greedy. She always has been. There was that incident with the jellies at her fifth-birthday party.' (I had no idea, and I doubt that the others had, of what she was talking about.) 'It's been the same ever after. Why do you think she married Aberdeen Angus? Also, I'll need to keep in her good books: I'll probably be relying on her for pin-money.'

'But what makes you think she'd want to live in The Graylings?' said Howard. 'Aberdeen A has a fancy job in New York.'

'Sarah doesn't need to live here. If she owns the house, she can sell it.'

'So are you saying we'll all have to move out?' whimpered Bunny. 'Oh dear!'

There was a rhubarb of anxiety.

'Not if Sarah never finds out that her father has died.' Amelia paused again. The silence was tense. 'I've thought about this a long time.'

'Don't be stupid, dear,' said Barbara. 'She's obviously going to find out, with probate and everything.'

'I'm not being stupid,' Amelia replied with corrosive politeness. 'I'm saying we don't tell *anyone* that Bernard has died.'

There was another silence, longer and tenser. This was a surprise from the vague and scatty Amelia, but even the vague and scatty sometimes achieve clarity when their vital interests are at stake.

The silence was broken by Dennis, who said, 'You can't conceal a death. It must be illegal for all sorts of reasons: failure to register, failure to pay tax, fraudulent drawing of a pension —'

'Depends what you mean by "can't", old boy,' said Roland. 'There's precedent in Gogol.'

'I mean it's illegal. And whether or not it's illegal, it's impractical. What happens when Bernard's signature is needed for something?'

Amelia emitted a tinkly laugh. 'Darling, I've been forging his signature for years.' We were all taken aback by this: Amelia has always been such a goody two-shoes.

'But it's bound to come out eventually,' I said. 'How are you going to explain Bernard's invisibility? What happens when Sarah and Angus come to visit?'

'They only come once a year. Bernard was away golfing last time. They didn't ask any questions.'

'It buys us time, I suppose.'

'We don't need much,' said Roland. 'We'll all be dead in a year or two.'

Dennis was becoming impatient. 'Jesus Christ! What about the body?'

'We bury him ourselves,' Amelia replied.

'*Who* buries him? *Where?*'

'Well, I suppose we'll all have to help. He can go by the pets.'

Along the path in the shrubbery there is a row of graves for the animals that the Bankeses used to have when Sarah was a child: the little tombstones are engraved with such unimaginative epitaphs as 'Hamish (1965-1974): a good fellow'. There's room for another grave, for when Sarah left home Amelia and Bernard got fed up with pets, and the only ones now in the house are Jeeves and Moth — respectively the responsibilities of Bunny and Barbara. I'm sure Amelia has no intention of admitting either animal, when its time comes, into the pantheon of Hamish and his colleagues.

'I'm having nothing to do with this,' Dennis asserted. 'We'll all end up in gaol.'

'Best place for you,' said Joy, who till then had been abstractedly playing an imaginary piano in the air with her left hand. It was unclear whether her 'you' was singular or plural.

'If we don't do it,' said Roland, 'we'll end up homeless. Which do you prefer?'

Dennis drummed his fingers on the arm of the sofa. 'We won't be homeless – we'll just have to make our own arrangements.'

'All very well for you,' said Howard. 'Your arrangements will be luxurious. I'll be in the doss-house.'

I said, 'You can have the pallet next to mine.'

Howard crooned 'Make Me a Pallet on the Floo-oor', until told to shut up.

'Anyway, The Graylings is our home,' said Bunny. 'We're a family now.' It was sad but true.

'We can't spend long debating this,' I said. 'If we're going to do it, we'll need to get him out of sight.'

Dennis now turned on me. 'I must say I'm surprised at you. Call yourself a legal theorist. If this sort of squalid ruse is what sixty-odd years of theorising results in, I don't know why you bothered.'

'And I suppose that, in all your years as a City solicitor, you never had to push the limits of the rules in order to secure your clients' squalid purposes?'

'I didn't break the law, and I didn't advise anyone else to. Anyway, solicitors are meant to be pragmatic: theorists are supposed to deal in principles.'

'One can make a principle of pragmatism,' said Roland.
'William James –'

'Another time, Roland,' I said. 'We've got to decide
whether we're going to follow Amelia's plan. Let's vote.'

The majority agreed to conceal Bernard's death. Dennis
wouldn't budge and the best we could get from him was
an agreement not to betray us. Barbara's support was luke-
warm: she had been unwontedly silent during the discussion – probably as a result of mixed motives. On the one
hand, she presumably wanted to continue to enjoy the
comfort of The Graylings; on the other, she is a reluctant
communard and would prefer Amelia to herself. This she
could achieve if Sarah booted them both out and they
moved into a house together.

The need to dispose of the corpse was, as I had urged,
pressing. The pets' burial avenue was conveniently located
for a discreet operation, for it is near the herb garden and
the area is screened by a thick row of shrubs. Howard and
I, as the fittest males of the company, were 'volunteered'
to do the digging, so we raided Mr Shanks's shed for two
spades, a fork and a pickaxe. I raised the question what
would happen if someone found us digging, and Howard
suggested saying that it was part of an exercise routine.

I don't know whether you have ever tried digging a grave,
but it's back-breaking work: the ground was waterlogged,
so the soil was heavy and stuck to the spade, and just underneath the surface there was a tangle of roots. One might
have hoped that Howard, who claims to enjoy exercise,
would rise to the challenge, but I did most of the digging
and his main contribution was to get in the way. The skill

of appearing busy while doing bugger all may have been something he picked up in the civil service. While this was going on, the others, with the exception of Dennis and Joy, kept watch from vantage-points around the compass. There was a nasty moment when Segunda emerged from the back door with some vegetable peelings for the compost heap, which is close to the herb garden: Barbara startled her by leaping out from behind a bush and insisting on carrying the peelings the rest of the way. Segunda is going to take some managing if we are to keep her off the scent.

It was nearly lunchtime when Howard and I, both grimy, sweating like pigs and wheezing, had finished the hole. It was only three foot deep, but we were whacked and time was short. We called the others from their lookout posts for a brief conference, and it was agreed that we would drag Bernard from the herb garden to the grave on some plastic sheeting which I had noticed in the shed. None of us wanted to touch the corpse, and Roland was the quickest to excuse himself: 'My bones aren't up to Bernard's bones, I'm afraid. Since you two are so well stuck in already, you'd better finish the job.' Howard and I rolled Bernard on to the sheeting and hauled him to the grave-side. Amelia requested that we tip him in without the sheeting, as he was biodegradable but it wasn't: Mr Shanks, she said, would take a dim view of our spoiling the soil with plastic. I had my doubts, for Mr S is pretty free with his rubbish – an almost empty bottle of Armillatox (Bunny calls it 'Armadillox') was lying nearby – and in any case Amelia's concern struck me as disproportionate: Mr Shanks's view would doubtless be a lot dimmer if he found Bernard in the soil.

The others returned to their posts, but it had been agreed that Amelia should be allowed to remain so as to pay her last respects: she maintained her chilly ataraxia as Howard and I rolled Bernard into the hole with a splash – for water had collected in it while we were fetching him. Being made of stuff less stern than Amelia's stuff, I shuddered when I realised that Bernard was floating. To obscure this demeaning spectacle, Howard and I shovelled back the sticky earth as fast as we could while Bernard stared at us, as if in outraged astonishment, as the soil went over his face and into his gaping mouth. When the hideous process was complete, we summoned the others to view the result – a tumulus about a foot high, sticking out starkly from the surrounding grass.

'Mr Shanks can hardly miss that,' said Bunny. 'What are we going to say?'

'Amelia kindly agreed to bury a friend's big dog,' Howard suggested.

Me: 'We'll need another tombstone, so that it blends in.'

Roland: 'Here lies Kierkegaard: a gloomy old cuss, but a Great Dane.'

'Bernard was proud of what he'd made of The Graylings,' I said. 'It should be: Si monumentum requiris, circumspice.'

'If you want the Monument, take the Circle Line,' said Howard.

We trooped indoors for lunch, after which I had a long nap to recover from my performance as First Gravedigger. When I awoke, I was rigid.

Chapter 5

•

Breakfast this morning started on a risqué note when Joy entered the dining-room without her skirt, displaying (1) legs flamingo-thin but polar-bear-white and (2) a large brown patch on the *outside* of her knickers, and had to be ushered from the scene by Dennis to make another and better-prepared entrance. Segunda is usually motherly on such occasions, her motherliness being on the cloying side for my taste. 'There you go,' she will say in an infant-teacher's voice when she hands you a cup of tea, as if you were some drivelling old fool who needed to be jollied along. Roland finds the phrase and its intonation as irritating as I do: '*Where* precisely am I going?' he retorted recently. In reply she blinked slowly like an owl and beamed at him indulgently.

This morning at breakfast, however, there was none of Segunda's usual placid and kindly good cheer. Pans and plates were clattered and Radio 1 was on extra-loud. Our feigned failure to notice this behaviour only made it worse, so Dennis tried some soothing conversation in the course of which he asked her what she was going to make for lunch.

She pursed her lips and continued doling out bacon — some of it flabby, the rest carbonised. Finally she said gnomically: 'How know I what lunch when food in the cupboard I put roamin the chambers.' She banged the coffee-pot down.

'Has something gone missing, Segunda?' Amelia asked.

There was some more banging before Segunda replied, 'Is missing Cuthbert.'

She folded her arms, like Ena Sharples, and stood glaring along the table at us all. We looked sheepishly down at our plates and played with the horrible bacon.

'Cuthbert for Dreyfus,' Segunda said more sternly.

There was a long pause. Then Roland said, 'Cuthbert's custard.'

We smiled and sighed, as at an inspired guess at a crossword, but were still baffled by Dreyfus. Dennis plucked up the courage to ask.

'DREYFUS!' Segunda shouted. 'Dreyfus, with esponge, Cuthbert, cream an' almendras.'

'Trifle!' we delightedly cried in unison.

'Oh dear,' said Bunny. 'I used some of it for the treacle pudding the other day. I'm sorry, Segunda. But there was plenty left in the tin for Drey-, um, trifle.'

'Is empty the tin,' Segunda replied in the voice of the Commendatore. 'Is in pedalo [the pedal bin].'

The plot thickened: someone had been in the custard since the emptying of the pedalo yesterday evening. All eyes turned to Howard, who was suddenly enthralled by *Guardian Woman*. When the silence became too much for him he looked up with an air of concentration distracted.

'Sorry?' he said.

'Custard,' Barbara said to him in the manner of the beadle in *Oliver Twist*.

Howard smiled as if uncomprehendingly.

'Custard,' Barbara repeated in the same manner. 'Have you been at it?' She might have been talking to Moth.

Roland said, 'My guess is it was Colonel Mustard with an iron bar in the library.' Individually his quips are amusing, but collectively they wear you down.

Segunda was still glowering at the end of the table, her arms now akimbo, her chin lifted. I thought of camels, whose noses are higher than their eyes.

Howard, never at his best in the morning, collapsed under the interrogation and blurted out the truth. 'For God's sake, all right, so I had a spot of custard in the night. It's not a crime to be hungry. We're not schoolchildren and Barbara isn't matron. I'm as entitled as the next man to have a little something.'

A simple confession would have been more dignified than this peevish attempt at self-justification, which bespoke a guilty conscience. He pushed the rest of his bacon aside (perhaps he was still full of custard) and got up from the table, farting loudly as he did so. The fart may have been involuntary, but was more likely an act of defiance, for Howard often farts deliberately, sometimes fluttering the tails of his jacket with his hands for what he takes to be comic effect. (His claim not to be a schoolchild is thus in doubt.) A few minutes later we saw him through the window: the morning mist was thick, so he was hard to make out, but he appeared to be goose-stepping from one end of the lawn to the other. When he reached the far end, he turned round and came back, at a trot this time. This – the exercise he had mentioned when I reprimanded him for using the Escalope – is his latest fad, aptly called fartlek.

Due straight after breakfast was our 'management meeting', a monthly event established by Barbara, who produces terse agendas which she needlessly circulates a week in advance, as if we were busy directors of some multinational. Today's agenda — as usual in a gigantic font size, the word-processing equivalent of green ink — said:

BERNARD
FRIDGE

Barbara styles herself the secretary at these meetings and Amelia, as châtelaine, is 'chair'. Amelia is not up to the job, for she is deaf, she fails to control the participants' tendency to ramble, which she shares, and her interventions, like her conversation in general, are subject to absent-minded tailing-off. Our discussions at the meetings therefore tend to peter out into vagueness or irrelevance.

We had assembled in the drawing-room and were waiting for Howard to come in from fartlekking so that the meeting could start. After some banging on the window by Barbara, he appeared: his face was crimson, zigzag veins stood out on his temples and he was breathing heavily and sweating liberally. Regrettably he squashed next to me on the sofa and kicked off his loafers, which had attracted grass and moss between welt and flapping sole. The socks were the ones he had on the other evening — and doubtless all intermediate evenings — only this time it was the other foot whose toes were bare: this I could tell from the big toe's having a nail. Despite his shortness of breath he pulled out a Hamlet and started rummaging in his jacket for matches, an exercise that caused me to bounce up and down on the sofa. Most of the matches in the box he eventually produced had, as he found by examining them seriatim (this required further rummaging, for his glasses), already been struck, and the virgin one he managed to unearth was unlightable because the side of the box was worn. After repeated strikings the match broke in half, the useful end shooting under the sofa. Howard got down on his knees and made windmill-swings of his arms under the sofa, retrieving an ancient chocolate but no match. This long distraction prompted an outbreak of conversation, as when there's a delay at the theatre just before curtain-up. Amelia tried to call the session to order, but so genteelly as to have no effect.

'For Christ's sake, can we start!' roared Barbara with better results.

'Bless yor,' said Amelia to Barbara. She says this a lot, whether or not anyone has sneezed.

Howard forlornly put the Hamlet back in his pocket and we turned to item 1: Bernard – a topic that had not been properly aired since the hasty burial. The question, obviously, was how best to explain his disappearance.

'We don't want to start giving a lot of excuses,' I said. 'We're bound to trip over them sooner or later. I think the best course is vagueness: if someone asks where he is, we just say we don't know – we think he's away. Even you presumably can subscribe to that, Dennis.'

Dennis had not come round to the scheme. 'Now the champion of clear and distinct ideas is advocating vagueness,' he grunted ill-humouredly. I was tiring of these jibes about my integrity: he, after all, was free-riding while the rest of us got les mains sales.

Amelia said, 'That's all right as far as it goes, but it won't do for me. I need some explanations up my sleeve.'

Barbara proposed that we help Amelia by making a list. Barbara likes lists. We came up with the following, to be selected according to circumstances:

- He's gone to London for a meeting.
- He's gone golfing with Biffy.
- He's in hospital – nothing too serious, so no need to visit.
- He thinks he deserves a cruise, so he has gone off on one.

Bunny piped up: 'How about: he's dead!'

'That suggestion,' Barbara replied as despairing looks abounded, 'doesn't inspire confidence.' Bunny's face dropped as the penny did.

Roland started being silly. 'We could say he's been transformed into a donkey. It happened in Apuleius.'

Inspiration was running dry, so we decided to round off with:

- I can't think where he has got to.

I was worried about Segunda. 'She comes in most days. She cooks the meals and tidies the rooms – Amelia's and Bernard's in particular. She can't fail to notice that Bernard isn't around.'

Bunny suggested sacking her, but this was greeted by howls. Howard's were particularly loud (we know why).

'We'll have to rely on her lousy English,' said Roland. 'Amelia will just have to say slowly, "Mr Bankes is away," and nod and smile a lot.'

'Her English may be lousy,' I replied, 'but she's no fool. She'll wonder why he's always "away".'

We could think of no alternative to letting her wonder.

Barbara said, 'I don't like to mention this, but there's also Joy.' Joy throughout the discussion had been staring gormlessly at the door handle. She continued to do so.

'What's that supposed to mean?' said Dennis.

'Come on, Dennis, we all know the bag of marbles is almost empty. She could come out with anything.'

Howard said, 'If she blurts something out, we'll put it down to the missing marbles.'

Joy turned sharply from the door handle to Howard. 'I'm not an idiot, you know. I'm perfectly well aware of what you're up to.'

'Of course, my dear, I wasn't inferring –'

'*Implying*,' said Roland.

Dennis cut this bit of the discussion short. 'I think Joy and I know how to behave ourselves,' he said brusquely, meaning that he knew how to keep her under control.

Before the agenda's other item, FRIDGE, Barbara managed to insert a discussion of the larder, on account of the Dreyfus case at breakfast. She began with a homily to the effect that, since Segunda is charged with cooking and shopping for us, she must be able to keep track of what is in stock. She paused and looked over her spectacles, first at

Bunny, then at Howard, on whom she fixed her gaze as she said, 'If people with no control over themselves see fit to thieve, we all take the consequences.' The phrase 'see fit' occurs often in her rebukes.

'Cuthbertless Dreyfus, oy vey,' said Roland.

Howard exploded. 'Thieve!' The zigzags came back on his temples and his face puffed up. I noticed that it was so fat these days that the arms of his glasses pressed into the flesh.

'I think we all get the message,' interposed Dennis with a nicely judged mixture of the brisk and the emollient. 'Shall we move on?' He should chair these meetings, but understandably has never volunteered.

Unfortunately the fridge proved a hotter topic. Everyone already knew the problem and there was no need for a decision – just for a renewed determination to keep to one's own shelf and have an eye on sell-by dates. Part of the trouble is that the village shop has a special shelf marked PAST SELL BY DATE, containing rotting foodstuffs at prices Tesco charges for their fresh counterparts. It is easy, but dangerous, to draw the invalid inference that the goods on the other shelves *aren't* past their sell-by date.

Barbara, however, would not let go of the egg incident last week. 'What the hell did you think those Bs were on the eggs for?' she said to Bunny, her head quivering with indignation. 'Do you think they put them on at the factory? Only a blithering idiot would fail to understand the eggs were somebody else's property.'

Bunny was close to tears.

'And only a bloody neurotic miser would go around

marking eggs,' retorted Howard, who had not forgiven her for 'thieve'. The sweat on his face, caused by the fartlekking, had reduced to a gleaming layer of grease.

'If it's me you're referring to in that insulting way –'

'As to who's being insulting –'

'*If* you'll allow me to finish – I don't *go around* marking eggs.'

'You go around making everybody miserable,' said Joy. She has these moments of acuity.

'What oft was thought but ne'er so well expressed,' said Roland.

Chapter 6

•

Adrenalin levels are high, as Sarah and Angus have come for their annual visit. They always come in mid-autumn, to get the trip out of the way before Thanksgiving and Christmas, which they like to spend at home. Angus is a banker on Wall Street, working in the American branch of Bernard's old firm: he met Sarah, 25 years ago now, when he was working in the London office and Bernard, thinking him a bright spark, had him round to a party. Bright he may be qua banker, but he's a standing joke among the communards, who like to imitate him. It takes little, whenever his name is mentioned, to get someone droning, 'Halloooo, I'm Aberdeen Angus. I'm a vurry borring mun,' the r's being rolled in the manner we assume, from pure prejudice, to be characteristic of Aberdonians. Angus, although from Aberdeen, does not roll his r's, but he is a very boring man.

Sarah is a financial journalist. It follows from her success in this field that she is good at unearthing facts that people want to conceal – a dispiriting thought, given the important fact that we all want to conceal from her and the literal unearthing that we want to avoid. It's clear that she has the inquisitorial skills necessary for the job: her idea of conversation is to give you a grilling. This invariably starts with an accusatory 'So'.

'So,' she said to me over lunch, in the mid-Atlantic accent that she has acquired in the seven years they have been in

New York, 'you're still writing that tome on the conceptual foundations of contract law. What do you say to those critics who hold that it doesn't have conceptual foundations but is just a hotchpotch of doctrines dreamt up for the nonce?'

Although she speaks softly, she always manages to convey that she thinks you're a fool. Now that she is 50-ish, she wears half-moon spectacles for close work: these she uses to effect in her interrogations, peering over them sternly with the pale blue eyes that she inherited from her father. The physical resemblance to Bernard is upsettingly close: if Sarah were bald, the likeness would be uncanny. The only touch of Amelia about her is the large chin.

Having mangled me, she turned to Amelia, and the inevitable happened. 'So, where is Dad? He wasn't here when we came last time. I'm beginning to think he hates me as much as you do.'

'I don't hate you: don't say such dreadful things. I've told you, Daddy is – ah...'

She petered out. God knows, she had been well enough rehearsed. We had agreed that the line Amelia would take was that Bernard had had to go at short notice to Liechtenstein, where he used to be a trustee of some investment vehicle or other. The Liechtenstein connection had slipped our minds when we were making the list of alibis, so we added it later. Now Amelia's mind had gone blank: her vagueness and dodgy memory were always mildly irritating, but they have become a serious threat. I was tempted to help her out, but it had been agreed that the rest of us would say as little as possible about Bernard's whereabouts, to avoid the risk of conflicting statements.

She recovered as best she could. 'Oh Lord, I can't remember where he's gone. He's always off somewhere or other.'

'We don't make these visits for fun,' Sarah said. 'We come over to visit both of you. We give you enough notice, surely.' She paused and peered keenly over her half-moons at Amelia. 'There's nothing wrong, is there? He hasn't left you or anything?'

'Don't be ridiculous.' Amelia laughed brittly. Her hand was shaking as she took some custard.

Bunny remonstrated, 'Bernard was always devoted to your mother.'

'God help us,' muttered Roland as Sarah, doubtless about to probe the 'was', swivelled her hawk-like gaze towards Bunny. I felt sweat on my palms.

Suddenly Howard started thumping the floor violently with one foot. He looked like a bison about to charge. 'God Almighty – terrible cramp! Do excuse me.'

The distraction showed unusual presence of mind on Howard's part. The rest of us waded in with strenuously solicitous advice. 'Wiggle your foot around like this,' said Barbara, pushing her chair back to demonstrate and displaying one of her purple bunions. She likes to go unshod.

The ruse worked. By the time the chimerical cramp had abated, the conversation had moved on.

'How long do you think you'll be able to keep this up?' Dennis murmured to me drily as we went into the drawing-room for coffee.

Chapter 7

•

No-one has liked to say anything, but for some time Joy has been a bit pongy at the back. (The glimpse we all received of the stain on her pants has been mentioned.) There is probably a connection between this phenomenon and my recent sighting of Dennis hurriedly carrying a bundle of sheets into the utility-room: bed-changing and laundry are usually Segunda's domain, but I suspect Segunda willingly agreed to delegate this bit of work. We were not surprised, therefore, when Dennis announced yesterday that Joy was to go into hospital next week for an operation on, as he put it, her bum. Everybody wanted to ask for details, but no one ventured to, as Joy was present and we couldn't be sure how much she had been told or had retained. Joy was, however, taking no part in the conversation, her attention being absorbed by a very simple jigsaw depicting some firemen in front of their engine.

'These men have come to mend the roof,' she said to me conspiratorially when I showed a polite interest. Her eyebrows were magenta, for she had used lipstick instead of a pencil.

Joy is no longer able to cope with games that are more demanding, such as Scrabble. When we moved in, she was better at it than I, but her spelling became increasingly heterodox. I challenged 'peni', which made her angry, but for the sake of peace I conceded it after Roland, who was kibitzing, defended it as a Spenserian form. When Joy started making words go diagonally, or both vertically and horizontally, I decided that further games were pointless.

Dennis looked worried as he told us that Dr Pee had found a lump. I don't envy Pee this side of his job, but he seems to relish anal work. When I last visited him he said that while I was there he might as well check my prostate. He instructed me to drop my trousers and pants and to curl up in a foetal position on the couch. Donning a rubber glove which he had lubricated with Vaseline, he pushed his middle finger, more vigorously than I would have chosen, up my bottom.

'Have you ever had this done to you before?' he asked, possibly sensing my tension.

'I did go to public school,' I heard myself reply.

Since I was facing the wall, I couldn't tell from his face whether he enjoyed this mot, but no chuckle was audible. Perhaps he had heard them all before, or perhaps, coming from Singapore, he didn't understand. When he drew his finger out, it was like the involuntary expulsion of a large stool. I found the whole process rather pleasurable and wondered whether, unlike tickling, it was something you could do to yourself. I have never got round to trying.

Where was I? Joy's lump – yes.

Dennis went on, 'We won't know whether it's serious till she goes under.'

'You could do with a rest,' said Bunny, tactlessly but truly, for Dennis looks frayed. The other night I heard him shouting at Joy.

'I don't know what I'd do without her,' he said too softly for Joy to hear even if her attention should wander from the jigsaw. His eyes were pink and glistening behind his spectacles, which had gone slightly misty.

With this on his mind, Dennis was in no state to face the first of the two dramas of the evening. Because of his arthritis he owns a sort of electric tricycle, called a Gadabout, which enables him to tootle down to the village when his hip is playing up. A liberation for their users, Gadabouts are a menace to others: they are allowed on the pavement because they are supposed to go at walking pace, but in fact they zoom along and people little more mobile than the drivers have difficulty leaping from their path. If a Gadabout went over your foot, it would break 20 bones, and if it hit you head-on it would be curtains. Dennis however is a sedate and considerate driver – he guards against collisions by squeezing a large Mr-Toad-style horn – and was therefore infuriated when a fortnight ago Amelia accused him, coram the rest of us, of straying on to the lawn with his vehicle. The accusation was the more exasperating for being made with the saccharine politeness that Amelia adopts when she intends to be unpleasant.

'Mr Shanks takes a dim view of it,' she said. 'He'd just done the edges. We did a full 360 degrees before I managed to placate him.'

Mr Shanks doesn't like to look you in the eye and therefore stands at an angle when you are talking to him. You try to square up, he moves round, and so on until, if the conversation is long enough, you have boxed the compass.

Bunny went to Dennis's defence. 'Couldn't the tyre marks have come from Oik's dreadful motorbike? You know what he's like.'

'Oh no, I think not,' Amelia cooed. 'You see, there were three tracks and Oik's bike only has two wheels.'

Dennis had suspected for some time that someone had been borrowing the Gadabout without his permission: when he went to fetch it from the garage, it was not quite in the right place and had spatterings of mud. He is a precise and orderly man and notices these things. The suspicion was now confirmed, and he was damned if he would put up with being falsely accused of the joyrider's inability to steer. He had sued on behalf of clients where less, in point of justice, was at stake. Interrupting his cooking (it was his night), he said, 'Someone in this room knows very well that they have been using my Gadabout and are responsible for the damage to the lawn.'

He turned sternly to Howard, who responded with an I-haven't-the-faintest-idea-what-you're-on-about gaze.

'All right, then,' Dennis continued, 'no-one is going to get any supper till the culprit has owned up.'

The headmasterly dignity of the message was undermined by the fact that he was wearing Bunny's naked-Venus apron and brandishing a grill-pan of sausages. Although he was using both hands, his wrists are so weak that he could barely keep hold of the pan, which was wobbling. He had to put it down.

There was silence. Looks were exchanged, many of them with Howard. During the stand-off the baked beans on the stove started to crackle.

'The culprit may be too embarrassed to confess in front of everyone,' I suggested. 'Perhaps you could relax your stance sufficiently for us to proceed with the sausages. I'm sure the miscreant will come and have a quiet word with you later.'

I didn't believe this, but I was hungry. Although the proposal was widely supported, Dennis wasn't happy: he took at least as dim a view of the situation as Mr Shanks did of the more limited matter of the tyre marks.

'If people want supper, they can serve themselves,' he said sulkily. 'I'm not bringing it to the table.'

He dished out portions of sausage and dried-up beans for himself and Joy, took them to the table and left the rest of us to fend for ourselves.

The culprit never came forward, but the crime was solved yesterday evening in the light of a more serious one. It being Roland's turn to cook, there was the usual exodus: Howard disappeared at dusk and Amelia and Barbara set off together for, respectively, opera and dance-and-movement. Barbara has taken to doing her homework in her room, which is next to mine: since she knows I hate to be disturbed, I view this as an act of war. She alternates between thundering and swishing: the thundering I recognised to be caused by the impact of her heels, but the swishing was more irritating because its cause was obscure. Concentration on the law of contract having become impossible, I went on to the landing and peered through her half-open door. She had rolled back the carpet and was swirling slowly round while saying 'One two three four', a rictus glued on her face as if she were a model in an ad for toothpaste. Her arms were outstretched and her bunion was tracing a circle on the floor. This was the source of the swishing. Hoping she got a splinter in it, I slammed her door behind me.

In the absence of Howard, Amelia and Barbara, the rest of us were treated to Roland's Unbeatable Gammon Delight. The 'b' should have been omitted and our only delight was in clearing the muck away and moving on to ice-cream, which we assumed was beyond Roland's powers of buggering up – wrongly, for he had failed to take it out of the freezer early enough and we were unable to penetrate it for a quarter of an hour. 'Take your pick,' Dennis gamely quipped.

This ordeal over, we went into the drawing-room, where we usually watch telly after supper; but Roland imposed the radio, as he wanted to hear a play by Beckett. It was a good way of preparing for bed: by the end, Bunny's eyes were rolling upwards, her neck muscles momentarily slackening and her head accordingly lolling sideways or dropping forwards with a jolt. Dennis, who was sound asleep, woke himself with a snore as Roland was switching the radio off.

'I wasn't asleep,' Dennis slurred, and then turned to Joy, who had been staring throughout at the blank screen of the television. 'Did you enjoy that, darling?'

'Not bad,' she replied, 'but the picture was poor.'

At that moment there was an extravagant crash outside, as if from *The Goon Show*. Jeeves, who had also succumbed to Beckett and until that moment had been asleep, twitching and quivering, on Bunny's knee, sprang to the floor and started a frenzied yapping.

'It's those black men,' said Joy with composure. 'There were five in the bathroom yesterday.'

Dennis, Bunny and I went to the window, pulled back the

curtains and peered into the night. All we could see was a light near the ground, pointing up at an angle and illuminating the branches of the pear tree.

Dennis, inspired perhaps by Joy's mention of black men, adopted the manner of an officer in *Zulu*. 'You ladies stay here. The men will go out and investigate.'

Roland, who had settled into a chair and was leafing through the TLS as if nothing had happened, was unenthusiastic about joining Dennis and me, but self-respect obliged him to.

Outside, the first thing we saw was Amelia, sitting on the ground and looking dazed. Beside her was an overturned dustbin. Barbara was stalking around, peering at the surface of the drive with a torch. Then we identified the source of the angular light: it was the headlamp of Dennis's Gadabout, which was lying on its side. Beside it, Howard was clambering to his feet: when he had got himself up, he stood swaying like a poplar in a gale and grinning stupidly. Barbara shone the torch in our eyes and we froze in a row, our eyes averted, as if we were a bunch of hoodies caught nicking a motor-scooter.

'Don't just stand there,' she called. 'One of you take over from me looking for Amelia's glasses. Another of you pick up the dustbin and help me get her into the house. The third of you can deal with that buffoon.'

She was unusually free from stridency and I was struck by her businesslike manner, which was more authentic than Dennis's military impersonation. It crossed my mind that Barbara might be my choice for the desert island, even though not for the drawing-room or bedroom. Roland volunteered for the soft option of looking for the spectacles, a task to which the curvature of his spine suited him but which he soon abandoned on the basis that it was too dark and that 'we' could find them more easily in the morning. He then hurried back into the house. I picked up the scattered rubbish, righted the dustbin and then helped Barbara heave Amelia to her feet: she seemed shaken rather than damaged. Dennis, as owner of the Gadabout, elected to deal with the buffoon. Their voices were becoming louder as we went indoors.

The train of events was easily sorted out when we gathered – with the exception of Howard, who had gone to bed in disgrace – in the drawing-room to drink the Horlicks that Bunny had meanwhile been preparing (Amelia's was fortified with Rémy Martin). Howard had borrowed the Gadabout to go to the pub, drunk too much, driven home fast and unsteadily, failed – until too late – to notice Amelia and Barbara who were walking up the drive after their stint of adult education, and swerved to avoid them, toppling the vehicle with his great weight. Amelia had likewise toppled when jumping out of his way. Under questioning from Dennis, he had asked for other offences to be taken into consideration, viz. several previous borrowings of the Gadabout, including the one that had caused the tracks on the lawn.

'Disgraceful disrespect of property, and a threat to life and limb,' huffed Amelia, whose shock the brandy had modulated into indignation.

We hoped to sleep soundly after these alarms, but at two a.m. I heard crashing in the kitchen followed by thundering on the first-floor landing. It could only be Howard, still in his cups, on the hunt for custard or an equivalent. As I needed a pee, I went downstairs to investigate. I came face to face with Oik. He was carrying the carving fork, his eyes were goggling and he had a crazed grin (for a split second I thought of Barbara as she practised her dance and movement). The hair on my neck stood on end and my knees started to tremble.

His face six inches from mine, Oik suddenly yelled, 'This is the end of the world, old man. I'm the angel of death and you're the devil. You're the fucking devil, you fucking evil old cunt fucker, and these are the flames of hell.'

He had in his other hand a lighter, which he now flicked on just under my chin. The flame was two inches high. Shying away from it, I tottered back against the banister and, for the first time in 73 years, peed myself.

By this time, doors on the first floor had opened a chink. Joy's voice could be heard stage-whispering, 'The black men are outside.' I wished they had been, as they might have bounced Oik, who emitted a screaming laugh and – thank God – bounded downstairs. Others now ventured on to the landing. Although I was shaking all over, I hurried up to my room, mortified at the thought that they could see the sodden trousers of my pyjamas. There was also a patch on the landing carpet. When I got to the second floor I heard Howard snoring obliviously, but Barbara was standing at her door like the foul witch Sycorax. She was wearing not witch's costume, but a pair of flannel striped pyjamas, as if she had just romped out of the dorm with Jennings and Darbishire. In no state to deal with her 'What the hell's going on *now?*', I scuttled into my room, fumblingly yanked off my trousers and cleaned myself up. Then I sat on the bed, numb.

There was a whirr of the Escalope, then a clank and a gasp, then a scratch on my door. Without waiting for the 'come in' that would not have been granted, Bunny came in with a cup of fortified Horlicks, much of it spilt in the saucer on account of the Escalope's uneven motion. She waddled up to the bed and sat down beside me.

'I thought you'd rather have yours up here,' she said. 'The others are having their dose in the lounge. That's the end of the Horlicks: we'll get it in the neck from Segunda tomorrow, unless Oik's skewered her on the fork before then.'

I surprised myself by bursting into tears. It was mainly the shock, of course, but also the humiliation of the pee, and then a wave of misery about what the pee signified – the helplessness and hopelessness of old age – followed by a bigger, existential, wave: if it all comes to this, what's the point of ever having been young, or of living at all?

Bunny put her arm round me and gave me a kiss. 'It's all right, darling, he's gone now. That will teach us to be more careful about the back door. We forgot to push the bolt in the earlier excitement. Come on, why don't you climb into bed like a good boy.'

She was talking to me as if I were of an age at which it is acceptable to wet your pants. I meekly did as she told me, and she tucked me in.

'Goodnight, sweetheart.' She kissed me on the forehead, turned off the light and tiptoed out. The Escalope whirred again and I drifted off.

Chapter 8

•

As I feared, Segunda has started asking questions about Bernard. She has been told that he is 'away', but she has noticed that he has taken none of his things.

'It's a long story, Segunda,' I overheard Barbara saying. 'You shouldn't expect Mr Bankes to come back for a long time.'

It is unclear what Barbara thought she was doing. In the first place, she was departing from the agreement that, in order to minimise the risk of conflicting stories, the explanations of Bernard's whereabouts should be left to Amelia; in the second, the stuff about not coming back for a long time is not on the settled script of excuses. It may be that Barbara just can't resist meddling and thought that a broad statement of this sort was the best way to expel the matter from Segunda's mind, but her remark could be interpreted as indicating that she isn't fully behind the plan: perhaps her heart isn't in it, so that she doesn't consider her words carefully, or, worse, she is deliberately creating clues that will lead Segunda or someone else to realise what's going on. I had a bad feeling about Barbara, and decided to share it with the others.

An opportunity arose after tea this afternoon. Barbara was out somewhere – she hadn't appeared for tea – and Dennis was at the hospital with Joy, who was admitted earlier in the day and is due to go under the knife, or whatever they use for bottoms, tomorrow. Amelia, Howard, Roland,

Bunny and I were sprawled around the drawing-room, wondering how to fill the stretch of time before supper, so I went to the door, looked into the hall to check that no-one was around, then shut the door and returned to my seat. I was unsure how to proceed, for Amelia and Barbara are so thick with each other that criticisms of the latter are liable to alienate the former. One possibility was to speak so softly that Amelia wouldn't hear; but that would have defeated the object, a fortiori as Howard, whose hearing-aid has been playing up (it keeps whistling in that way which infuriates others but seems not to bother the wearer), probably wouldn't hear either. The best course seemed to be to approach the Barbara issue via some general remarks about the need for tight security.

'I think we need a quick word about the Bernard question. We've already had some pretty close shaves. We have to stay vigilant.'

'Mum's the word!' chirped Bunny.

I was irritated by this flippancy. 'Easy to say, Bunny, but you hardly kept mum when Sarah was here.'

'I never said a word!'

'You said Bernard *was* devoted to Amelia.'

'Well, he was.'

I took a deep breath. 'If you say *was*, it suggests he isn't any longer. Sarah would think something had changed.'

'Something *has* changed. He's dead, isn't he?'

'Yes, dear,' said Amelia, at her most syrupy. 'But we don't want anyone to know that, do we?'

'But I never said he was dead.'

'You ought all to know by now,' said Roland, 'that my

wife is irremediably stupid. I'd impose a rule of total silence on her, but she wouldn't be able to keep it.'

Bunny's tail went between her legs, so I was gentle with her: 'Just try to remember not to say anything that could excite suspicion, OK?'

'OK,' she mumbled, like a small child who had been told off.

'And Amelia, you've got to stick to your script. Once you have decided what the alibi is for the occasion, you must remember it and not deviate from it.'

'I do my best, darling, but my memory – well, it has never been my strong card.'

'It's not that we can rely on the others. For a start, you never know what Joy's going to say.'

'Dennis keeps control of Joy all right,' said Howard.

'Yes,' said Roland, 'but he isn't a paid-up member.'

Howard: 'I know he said he wasn't going to get involved, but he also said he wouldn't betray us. He's a man of principle.'

This last statement nettled me. When we had first been discussing whether to hide Bernard, Dennis had in effect not only accused me of flouting my principles – which ones, he had not bothered to specify – but claimed that this made a mockery of my whole career as a legal theorist. Now Dennis was being congratulated for his own bloody principles. 'No-one's denying Dennis's integrity,' I said brusquely. 'But not betraying shades into getting involved.'

'Too deep for me, that, old chap. We're not all legal pinheads.' I hoped he meant eggheads or wasn't applying the term to me.

'I've no doubt he won't go down to the police station and shop us,' I explained, 'but what if the police come here and start asking Dennis questions? Will he take not betraying to include lying for our sake? Being a man of principle cuts both ways: one of his principles is telling the truth.'

Roland: 'That principle doesn't extend to telling the homicidal maniac where the axe is.'

'I'm afraid you're losing me,' said Amelia.

Me: 'We can't make Dennis change his position. I'm just saying that the active members have to be all the more careful.' It was time to move on to the thornier matter of Barbara. After a pause, I continued: 'I also have to say that I'm uneasy about Barbara.'

I picked up 'I have to say' from an old colleague. It means 'I don't have to say this, but I'm going to anyway, and you aren't going to like it.'

'Barbara's one of us, I can assure you,' Amelia said crisply.

I explained the grounds for my unease – not only her words to Segunda, but her tepidness when we had agreed on the plan to hide Bernard.

'But Barbara's not going to betray us,' said Amelia. 'Why on earth would she?'

I couldn't reply, 'Because she's a closet dike who would like you to herself and the rest of us to fuck off. She could achieve this by getting Sarah to take over The Graylings, kick us out and install you in a dower-house, where Barbara could join you.' So I settled for: 'I don't think she's as committed to the commune as the rest of us are.'

'That's not true. And even if it were, what reason would she have to betray us?'

I was fumbling. I should not have raised the issue without first having devised a form of words that would persuade Amelia without offending her and, second, having thought out a proposal which I could put forward for dealing with Barbara. I lamely said, 'At least can I suggest that you have a quiet word with Barbara to stiffen her resolve. If she knows you're committed, she's more likely to toe the line.'

'But she does know,' Amelia replied. 'I was the one who started this scheme, wasn't I?'

'Let's call a spade a spade, shall we?' said Howard. 'Barbara likes making mischief: it keeps her adrenalin up.'

'Oh really!'

I cast Howard a look imploring him to pipe down, but he negligently or wilfully failed to see it.

'No, I'm sorry, Amelia,' (he was getting louder) 'that woman is the rotten apple in our basket. She doesn't care a row of beans for the rest of us. I'd not put it past her to spill the beans just for the hell of it.'

I momentarily wondered whether the spilt beans were the same as the ones in the row. Howard lacks the instinct of self-preservation: it could not conceivably have been in his interest to offend Amelia in this way. It's inaccurate to say that he speaks first and thinks later: usually he speaks and never gets round to thinking at all.

Roland said, 'If Barbara grasses, she'll be in a lot of trouble herself.'

'She's wily enough to wriggle out of it. Barbara will go to the rozzers, tell them we've been hiding Bernard and swear blind that she had nothing to do with it.'

I threw Howard another look, more exaggeratedly imploring this time, as the door of the drawing-room had opened and Barbara had stepped in. Howard failed to notice her entry because (a) he was talking too loudly, and was anyway too deaf, to hear the door open and (b) he had his back to it. His harangue over, he looked around at the rest of us: we were all gawking guiltily over his shoulder at Barbara. Like a walrus on a rock, or Rita Hunter playing Brünnhilde as she awakens to greet the dawn, Howard eased his great mass round to see what we were staring at. He found Barbara glaring at him.

Roland dropped his eyes to the carpet, smiled sardonically and murmured, 'Oh whistle and I'll come to you, my lad.'

Amelia was the first to rally. 'Barbara, dear, the pot's a bit cold, but there are still some custard creams.'

Barbara didn't reply. She continued glaring at Howard: her lips were pursed in kissing formation, but there seemed little prospect of her giving him a kiss. The pursing accentuated her moustache. Then her glare swept the rest of us.

'I heard most of that,' she said icily (so she had been at the keyhole before she came in). 'I'm not going to rise to vulgar abuse. I'll just say this: if you want people to be trustworthy, you have to show them trust.' (I had heard some old bore voice the same platitude on *Thought for the Day* in the morning; Barbara must have been listening too.) 'If you don't trust them, you know what to expect. So: you're all on notice.'

She turned on her heel and stumped upstairs.

Chapter 9

•

I wish I had never toyed with that hypothesis about Dennis's queerness, for I now keep finding evidence for it. During Joy's stay in hospital, he seemed to spend half his time hanging around that psychopath Oik. And then – I can hardly bring myself to write this – I half-think that Dennis has an unhealthy interest in *me*. When we were sitting next to each other on the sofa, he rested his arm along the back behind me and patted my knee, leaving his hand there uncomfortably long and smiling too close to my face. At lunch my foot kept encountering his and, when afterwards I went to sit in the garden to make the best of the autumn sun, he startled me by looming up with a leer from behind a shrub. Could he have been incubating a desire in my direction all these years? Could that desire have started to show its ghastly face now that age is cracking inhibition and Dennis is finding himself increasingly lonely as Joy recedes into the dark? But isn't it supposed to be one of the few benefits of getting old that the libido lets you alone? You're no longer strapped to a lunatic, as some old Greek put it. I was never thus strapped, and on balance am glad of the fact, though I no doubt missed some fun. But then, perhaps this fretting about Dennis is a projection of *my* long-dormant and now-stirring libido?

I'm sure there's nothing in any of it. Dennis after all has had plenty of worries to distract him from sex. The day after Joy's operation a woman from the hospital appeared at the front door and asked to speak to Mr Dennis Middleton. She told Dennis that she was very sorry, but Joy had taken a sudden turn for the worse that morning and had died. Dennis hurried to the hospital, where he found Joy propped up in bed and as right, physically, as a trivet. It turned out that the hospital had two Joy Middletons on its books, the late one being a baby who had died after a 'life-saving' operation on the heart. The inefficiency of the hospital in identifying its patients was matched by its efficiency in disposing of their medical records: our Joy's had already been committed to the flames. Perhaps they contained nothing but sophistry and illusion.

Joy returned to The Graylings a couple of days ago, and the consultant's report on her condition, Dennis told us, would follow. She is up and about and, after her time away, even more disoriented than before. For some reason she has started straying up to the second floor and become convinced that my room is hers: one afternoon I walked in and found her asleep on my bed, like an effigy on a medieval tomb. Perhaps I'm irresistible to both halves of the Middleton ménage. I felt a faint stirring in my own loins, as I contemplated Joy's high cheekbones and still-full lips and the tracery of delicate veins under the translucent skin of her temples. The problem of Joy's invasions is hard to solve because my door doesn't have a lock: I have suggested at more than one management meeting that locks be fitted to people's rooms, but the idea has been vetoed by Amelia, who says she is not prepared to be forcibly excluded from any part of her own house. The feeble lock on the bathroom door is a dubious counterexample to that principle. When

I am inside my room I push a heavy chair against the door: that stops Joy from entering but not from rattling the door-knob, like a cat I got rid of years ago. When I'm out there's nothing I can do to stop her walking in, for the door opens inwards and the landing is devoid of anything big enough to block her way. I have therefore resorted to a Barbarous sign saying:

NO ENTRY: JOY, THIS IS NOT YOUR ROOM

Yesterday when I was coming upstairs I found Joy reading it slowly. Having done so, she started opening the door. At that moment Barbara emerged from her room. Neither of them had seen me, so I retreated a couple of stairs in order to watch.

Barbara made no effort to stop Joy. 'Are you going for a lie-down, dear?' she growled.

Joy replied, 'My husband's in there.'

'What's your husband called?'

Joy looked anxious, shook her head and didn't reply.

Barbara continued, 'And what's *your* name?'

Joy looked more anxious, gave Barbara a mournful look and shuffled into my room. Barbara turned to go down-stairs and encountered me. I pretended to have just been walking up. She passed by, saying nothing about Joy's having wandered on to my territory.

It's hard to interpret the incident favourably. A charitable view is that Barbara was using Socratic dialogue to elicit from Joy a recognition of the truth – but how did the questions about names assist the maieutics and why did she allow Joy to persist in her error? A more sinister reading, to which I incline, is that Barbara was deliberately confusing Joy, either with a view to hastening her departure to a home and thus weakening the cohesion of the commune, or out of sheer fiendish delight in tormenting the helpless.

I ushered Joy out, led her down to the floor below, where I gently propelled her in the direction of her own room, and then darted upstairs and into my room, dragging the chair in front of the door. I had just settled down to work when the Escalope started to whirr. The whirr increased in volume and pitch, there was a clank, a squawk, a half-second's silence, then a thump, then a 'Fucking Jesus fucking Christ' in Joy's most bell-like tone. I wondered whether it would be ethical to chain her to something.

Regrettably her operation has done nothing to reduce the smell from her backside: if anything, it's worse. Also a large turd was found near her usual chair in the drawing-room. The discovery was made just before tea, by Barbara, who stepped on it with her bare foot, squashing it into the rug. Barbara, swaying on one leg, roared to Segunda to come immediately with newspaper, cloth, brush and Domestos. Segunda was surly when she saw what she was expected to clean up, and she flounced from the room in fury when Amelia, who had come in with Bunny, started twittering about the damage that bleach would do to the rug – which had sentimental value as Amelia had bought it with Bernard on a holiday in Fez.

Barbara, now hopping towards the door, rounded on Amelia. 'It's not part of Segunda's normal duties to scrape human turds off the floor.'

'What do you mean, *human?*' Amelia replied.

As Joy and Dennis were just coming in, Bunny forestalled a hurtful allegation by saying, 'It must have been one of the animals.'

This attracted the lightning to herself. Barbara harrumphed, 'It must have been your dog, then. It certainly wasn't Moth: the turd's almost as big as he is.'

Her statement was true, but only doubtfully supported her conclusion, for Moth can eat a rabbit as large as himself: he starts with the ears, while the rabbit is still alive and screaming, and works his way through the lot – fur, bones and all – leaving only a small, bright-green organ: the spleen? Moth also persecutes Jeeves who, although small for a dog, is a lot larger than he, for Moth is a dwarf – a genuine one, not a rare breed: his tail is the size of a thumb and when he waddles on his stunted legs he looks like an animated tea-cosy. Barbara has tried to prevent spats between the two pets by putting up a timetable showing when each of them is allowed where in the house and garden. This document, which breaks the day into half-hourly segments, is ignored by both animals.

'Jeeves is a very good boy,' Bunny replied. 'He goes for at least two walks a day and he's perfectly house-trained.'

'Especially when it comes to food,' Barbara remarked drily.

This was an allusion to Jeeves's weakness for helping himself to food intended for the human residents. For breakfast Segunda sometimes puts a fry-up out on the hot plate, and on more than one occasion the first person down has found Jeeves, comfortably settled on the sideboard, working his way through sausages, bacon and eggs (he leaves the tomato). A while ago, when we went into the dining-room for Sunday lunch, we found Bunny having a furtive tug-of-war with Jeeves for the leg of lamb: he won and niftily dragged it out of the room and into the utility-room, where it took three of us to corner him and wrest the joint from his jaws. He met his nemesis a couple of weeks later when, again trying to drag the Sunday roast to somewhere more convenient, he fell from the dining-room table and ricked his back. For some time thereafter he walked crabwise.

Chapter 10

•

Howard's sleeping pattern is irregular, so I have recently been treated in the smallest hours to blasts of Mahalia Jackson, Eddie Condon and Dolly Parton, played through his gigantic speakers. My banging on the wall he either doesn't or pretends not to hear, so I have to climb out of bed, shuffle on to the landing and bash on his door till he emerges. More than once the noise I have made has woken Barbara, who has burst out in her Jennings pyjamas – once I caught an unwelcome glimpse of her pubic hair through the slit of the trousers – and reprimanded me as if I were the root of the problem. Howard's response is cunning: he is always deeply apologetic and claims that he didn't imagine the music could be heard outside his room. Even taking his deafness into account, the claim is risible, for the music is so loud that you can feel the vibrations through your feet. Then, while I stand there, he turns it very low – not off – and I go back into my room. As soon as I'm in bed, he turns it up again, not as loud as before but loud enough to prevent me from going back to sleep. If I'm angry enough, I get up again and demand that he turn the music off completely and finally, but usually I haven't the energy and I lie there tossing and turning.

My sleep is anyway fitful at the moment, for the Bernard matter is worrying me. At the time, Amelia's plan seemed attractive, if daring, and I was one of the ringleaders; but now, in the cold light of day, or rather the gloom of the small hours, the whole idea seems grotesque. I impatiently dismissed Dennis's strictures on my integrity, but I have to admit that he has a point. Apart from the ethics of the thing, there's the danger it has created for all of us. It's not as if the residents of The Graylings were a tightly disciplined cell: to cite just the biggest flies in the ointment, Barbara is flaky, Dennis is hostile, Joy is bonkers and Bunny is thick. What with Bunny's careless talk, we had a near miss when Sarah and Angus came to stay, and I foresee a series of nearer and nearer misses until eventually the whole crime – for there is no doubt it is a crime – comes to light. I can see the headline now in *Times Higher Education*: NOTED JURIST IMPRISONED FOR HIDING CORPSE. Perhaps there will be a picture.

To support this prediction, a courier has delivered an envelope addressed to Bernard and marked 'Strictly Private and Confidential: Addressee Only'. Amelia of course opened it and, the morning after my most recent nuit blanche, asked me to look at the letter it contained. Somewhere called Arkwell Hall was on the letterhead, and the text read:

Dear Bernard,

ARNOLDO & MICCOLUCCI S.r.L.

I am sorry to have to stir up some unhappy memories this far into your retirement. You will remember the highly regrettable difficulties the Bank got into with these people shortly before you left. I understand – it was before my time – that we managed to avoid scandal by buying them off for a very considerable sum.

I am afraid that I have now received a letter from Ercole Arnoldo alleging that, although the account has been settled between our two firms, there remain substantial liabilities on the part of those individuals who were directors of the Bank at the time. Five of the directors, including you of course, are still alive.

I am convinced that the allegation is without foundation, but I am sure you will agree that we need to decide together how best to deal with it. We on the Board are willing to lend whatever assistance we can to you and the other former directors, but, as Chairman, I am most anxious to avoid any further risk that the Bank's name gets dragged through the mud. I am sure I do not need to remind you of the suspected criminal connections – never proved, of course – of Arnoldo & Miccolucci. Poor Daddi's death was never satisfactorily explained.

I therefore propose that we meet, together with the Bank's lawyers, as a matter of urgency. To ensure complete confidentiality I suggest that the meeting take place not on the Bank's premises but here at Arkwell Hall. Would you therefore kindly let me know a few dates in the near future that might be convenient for you.

I am of course writing in similar terms to the other former directors.

Yours sincerely,
Anthony Benton-Sadie

It is an irony that 'Bernard has gone to a meeting' is one of
the alibis on our list of stand-bys. Bernard in fact stopped
going to them years ago: for a while after his retirement
he held some non-executive directorships which enabled
him to take home a few extra hundred thou in return for
dozing through the odd board meeting, but these had all
dried up by the time he hit 75. Now, suddenly, this Benton-Sadie character really did want Bernard at a meeting.
The request sounded pressing enough for it to be impractical for Amelia simply to ignore it, or even for her to keep
postponing the meeting's date. Moreover the letter was
worrying: it implied the existence of a serious threat to
those assets that it was the very purpose of our concealing
Bernard's death to enable us to continue to enjoy.

I advised Amelia to consult Dennis, who had been advis-
ing Bernard on just this sort of thing throughout his life;
but Dennis was snootily reluctant even to read the letter.
He repeated his refusal to have anything to do with our
plot.

'We're not talking about that, Dennis,' said Amelia. 'I'm
simply asking you to help me answer a business letter.'

'The fact that you're asking me is a consequence of the
plot,' Dennis tiresomely replied. 'And I'm sure the answer
you have in mind is one that will further your deplorable
aims.'

'As a lawyer,' I said, 'you should be prepared to entertain
distinctions. Even if this were a consequence of the plot, it

would be indirect enough for you to be able to give Amelia a bit of help without sacrificing your precious principles.'

'And, as a lawyer, *you* should have some respect for the law,' Dennis retorted primly before reluctantly agreeing to have a look at the letter. He pushed his glasses up on to his forehead and peered at the paper, holding it three inches from his nose. Dennis has been very short-sighted for as long as I have known him; in middle age he also became very long-sighted. I was sad to discover, first from his case and later from my own, that these conditions are not mutually exclusive.

As he read the letter, he started to look sick. 'Ah yes, I remember it well, as the old song goes,' he said when he had finished. 'We advised the bank: it was the worst job I ever did. The Italians were criminals – Mafia probably. An employee in the Bank's Milan office died: suicide or murder, it wasn't clear. Then the papers got hold of it.'

'It's a shame,' I said, 'that Amelia can't write back and say Bernard is dead. That presumably would get rid of them.'

'Amelia can and should say Bernard is dead, as I have repeatedly urged.'

'Spare us *that* old song. You could stand in for Bernard at the meeting: we could easily forge a power of attorney if one were needed.'

Dennis waved his arm in exasperation. 'Go to the meeting yourself.'

'I don't have experience of this sort of thing and I don't know the facts. You qualify on both counts.'

'Forget it. I'm not going anywhere near this.'

He hobbled out of the room, leaving us in our quandary.

The best I could advise Amelia was to write back that Bernard was away, that he thus could not attend a meeting, but that Amelia would pass on the letter and was sure Bernard would agree to whatever Benton-Sadie and his friends decided. To say merely that Bernard was away was to adopt the strategy of vagueness for which Dennis had taunted me when I had proposed it at the management meeting: it seemed the safest course in the circumstances. I was worried in particular that Benton-Sadie might try to track Bernard down via Angus: if Angus in turn set Sarah on the case, she would be more likely to catch us out if we supplied an alibi that was precise. As it is, she will be suspicious if she hears that Bernard is 'away' yet again.

Chapter 11

•

Nikki, the 22-year-old daughter of Sarah and Angus, has come to stay. She has pink hair, ironmongery in her face, and a panda's quantity of eye-shadow. Her stripy tights and very dirty Converse shoes typify her manner of dress. After leaving school at 16, she spent several years with no identifiable occupation: she was kept from starvation by the dole, occasional handouts from her parents and a small and erratic income derived from the walking of other people's dogs. She has a dog of her own, a giant poodle called Shazza, whom she brought with her, to the dismay of Jeeves and Moth. Although Shazza's tail has been pollarded in the usual way, so that it looks like a sprig of cauliflower, the rest of her coat has been tied into dreadlocks. Like her owner, she is untrained and unruly: on arrival she picked Moth up in her jaws and shook him violently. Moth got his revenge by biting Shazza's ankle when she was asleep.

Like us, Nikki lives in a commune, for which Amelia, with doubtful consistency, reproaches her. Whenever Nikki comes to stay, she gets a lecture about settling down with a nice boy. 'I don't see how you can bear to waste your time squatting in a condemned dump with a lot of drug-taking drop-outs,' Amelia said this time, in characteristically impartial language.

Nikki replied, 'So why's that worse than surrounding yourself with a lot of parasitic old wrecks? I bet you take more drugs between you than we do.'

The point was well taken, I thought, although I didn't care for the 'parasitic old wrecks' bit. The exchange developed into a row, as it usually does: the thing has become a ritual which grandmother and granddaughter seem to enjoy. Listening to Amelia and Nikki speak, it's hard to believe that they are closely related, the former's accent being that of a retired admiral, the latter's being Estuary: Nikki, like the Chinese, drops the 't' from any word that ends in it ('inni') and she has the full quota of dreary trendyisms, inflecting her assertions as questions and peppering her discourse with 'like'. The two of them share a tendency to tail off in mid-sentence, but in Amelia's case the cause is absent-mindedness, genuine or studied, while in Nikki's it is some mixture of boredom and laziness.

Amelia also likes to badger Nikki to 'do something in life' (another case of pots and kettles). Nikki used to retort, 'We're, like, human *beings*, right, not human *doings*?', but has now conceded that — as she puts it with cynical instrumentalism — she should 'get a CV'. The change of attitude may have been caused by fear of long-term destitution and isolation: her commune, I gather, is thinning out as its members do the settling down that Amelia recommends. Nikki's first step to the acquisition of a CV has been to sign up for two courses at a former poly, one on photography, the other on 'cultural studies'. Even though you don't need A-levels to get on to either (just as well for her), the latter course issues in a degree. I'm thinking of handing back my degrees in protest, as various codgers did their MBEs when The Beatles got that honour.

Roland is unable to contain himself on the topic of cultural studies. He is tiresomely smug at the moment, having been invited out of the blue to appear on Radio 3's *Private Passions* – a fact he keeps dropping into conversation. PP is the thinking man's *Desert Island Discs*: the difference is that, instead of Kirsty Young rushing you through your life and allowing you brief snatches of your old favourites, Michael Berkeley allows you to drone on for hours about yourself and your opinions and to play great swathes of stuff. Roland is threatening to ask for the whole of *Parsifal*.

He moved in for the kill at supper. 'Cultural studies, eh? Is it true that they were invented to give sociologists something to look down on?'

Nikki was not ready with a witty reply to this, so she returned a gaze of boredom and contempt.

Roland continued: 'And what do cultural studies study, Nikki? Culture, I suppose. So what is culture?' He turned to her in the manner of Paxman.

Nikki was cornered into saying, 'Man, everyone knows what culture is. It's, like, the way you live and think and so on. It's *popular* culture.'

'Ah yes, the mores of morons. So culture's popular culture. And by that definition popular culture is popular popular culture, nicht?' As he slowly twisted his head around at the rest of us in search of admiration, he resembled a tortoise peering out of its shell.

Nikki pursed her metal-encrusted lips and glared at her plate. Roland, getting into his stride, asked her to distinguish cultural studies from social anthropology, which she was unable to do, as she had not, it seemed, heard of social anthropology. Dennis suggested that soc anth was cultural studies applied to 'coloured people'. Howard suggested that we change the subject. Bunny, who was sitting beside Nikki, patted her and told her that Roland was only teasing – which made Nikki more surly, as she now felt that she was being treated as a child.

Roland, unwilling to let go, asked Nikki which authors the students were given to read. When she replied with the predictable list of Left Bank poseurs, he asked, 'And how do you decide which of their views – if views they can be called – is the correct one?'

'The true one's the one that's true for you, OK?'

'They told me, Protagoras, they told me you were dead. But it's good to know you're alive and spreading your poisonous and self-refuting relativism around the modern academy. So, if it's true *for me* that cultural studies are a pile of pretentious claptrap, then that's what they are – am I right? Or am I only right *for me*? Anyway, I think we've established that you don't need much culture to do cultural studies.'

Nikki started to cry. Supper having finished, Howard tried to cheer her up by inviting her to his room to listen to his blues collection. The invitation made me uneasy on two counts: first, that the music would keep me awake; second and more serious, that Howard might try to have his way with Nikki, which could outrage Amelia, if she ever found out, to the point of jeopardising Howard's continued residence here. I was wrong on the first point, right on the second. Despite the cheerless strumming of Blind Lemon, I managed to nod off, but I awoke an hour later to a muffled squealing through the wall, as of a pig being stuck. If I could be woken by this, so could Barbara, in which case it would get back to Amelia. I drowsed off and when I awoke again all was quiet. I got up to go for a pee, not bothering to put on my dressing-gown despite a robust stiffy that was forcing my pyjama trousers up like a pole in a wigwam. At the moment I went out on to the landing, Nikki emerged from Howard's room. (The sleeping Howard could be heard within, making a noise like a diesel engine.) She was naked apart from her pants: the rest of her clothes were draped over her arm, the stripy tights dancing like the legs of a puppet. My eyes flicked to her paltry and banana-like breasts – each had a ring through the nipple – and I felt my own banana get even stiffer. Her eyes flicked to it. We simpered at each other and she ventured a stupid excuse:

'I left my specs in Howard's room after the blues.'

'Make sure you don't bump into your grandmother on your way back to your room,' I whispered. 'And for God's sake don't let Barbara catch you up here.'

I pointed at Barbara's door and made a Shshshsh gesture with my finger to my lips. The thought appalled me of Barbara finding us on the landing, Nikki almost naked and me ithyphallic. Barbara would find it more than a bit ithy. We sneaked downstairs, to guest-room and bathroom respectively.

Nikki shows more promise as a photographer than as a cultural theorist (faint praise): the portfolio of work she showed us when she arrived – gritty black-and-whites of run-down streets, overgrown railway sidings and the like – was, to my untutored eye, accomplished and professional-looking. Amelia used her position of influence in the local community to arrange for a small exhibition of her grand-daughter's work to be included in the Arts and Crafts Fayre in the village hall. Nikki, wanting to add some portraits to her show, offered to photograph the residents of The Graylings. We protested mildly, but were vain and bored enough to be delighted, so the arm-twisting was perfunctory.

The shoot was fixed for the morning after her passionate encounter with Howard, so we were more dapper than usual when we appeared at breakfast: Joy had her skirt on and even Howard had combed some strands of hair over his bald patch, to bar code effect. The saloon – a grand, damp and cheerless room reserved for special occasions – was turned into a studio, and there we posed seriatim with various props: Amelia donned a fur stole that had survived the fire in the cupboard (a good choice, given the saloon's Siberian temperature (the radiators, having only recently been turned on, emitted a Nibelheimian clanking but no warmth)), Joy looked glamorous in a feather boa, Bunny pressed a reluctant Jeeves on to her knee, and Barbara wore a deerstalker, shooting-jacket and plus-twos. Years ago, during a brief phase of dandyism, I had a pair of these, but the itchiness of the woollen socks was unbearable and I had to admit that I looked a nana. Barbara looked even more of one.

On the day the Fayre opened we pushed past the primitive daubs produced by the WI, the even cruder clay pots by children from a nearby school for special needs, and the hassocks luridly embroidered by a Mrs Shagbolt, and made straight for the corner of the hall devoted to Nikki's work, where we expected to see ourselves transformed into Clark Gables and Greta Garbos, with wrinkles and blemishes smoothed away and perhaps some hand-tinting of cheeks and lips. But, as we should have predicted from the snaps of urban desolation and from the intensity of the lights pointed at us in the saloon, Nikki is a virtuoso of hard-edged realism. The pictures were too realistic for their subjects to be immediately recognisable: it only dawned on me that the moustachioed gnome perched on a sofa was Bunny when I identified the mysterious hairy mass around her knees as Jeeves, and it was hard for me to accept that I was the scraggy-necked, bespectacled lizard resembling Bertrand Russell in his late 90s. The least unflattering portrait was that of Roland – unjustly, given the pasting Nikki had got from him – whose face had an austere and etherial gravity (perhaps a beneficial spin-off from Parkinson's). We stood there in a line, silently confronting this evidence of our decay, before hurrying off in various directions to avoid looking each other in the eye. The exhibition has not been mentioned since.

Chapter 12

•

Of the two bathrooms in The Graylings one is larger and better appointed than the other, so we all compete for time in the good one. Barbara has tried, with a sign saying THERE ARE TWO BATHROOMS: IF THE BIG ONE IS OCCUPIED, USE THE LITTLE ONE, to prevent bottlenecks, but the trouble is that it's hard to tell when the big one *is* occupied, as the lock on its door is dodgy. The consequently frequent intrusions produce a now standard exchange along the lines of 'Ah – hallo – oop, sorry – shan't be long – no, no, take your time.' It's worth exposing yourself to this, for the little bathroom has severe defects, one being the bad cracking of the lavatory bowl. As a visiting plumber warned us, 'If it goes while you're going, you won't be able to stand up quick enough. You'll slice your arse bad enough for stitches.' He was a mild, middle-aged man called John Osborne: 'I'm an angry young man,' he murmured wearily before any of us had time to make quips. The bath in Bathroom Parva is also substandard: it is narrow and the rubber of its plug has perished, letting water seep away. As a result, Bunny once became wedged in the bath like a whale at low tide. Fortunately Roland was able to refloat her, but the rest of us had to stand by to lever her out if flotation couldn't be achieved. I was glad to be spared this, as I didn't relish the prospect of seeing Bunny naked and/or squeezing my fingers between the bath and her Michelin hips.

Bathroom Magna is much grander and boasts a jacuzzi, which Bernard installed in the '80s, when such things were a novelty. The jacuzzi is elliptical, six feet long and five wide, so not even Bunny could get trapped in it. I have never seen the attraction of these things. Apart from smacking of the nouveau riche, they make you – or at least me – feel faint when they are hot: perhaps it has something to do with the foam, which always seems to get out of hand. In any event, Amelia enjoys hers – or did until last week, when we heard her scream from the bathroom. She had filled the jacuzzi, switched on the pump, gone to her room to undress, returned to the bathroom and climbed in, and it was only when she was fully immersed that she realised she was lying next to Howard, who had been invisible under the bubbles (he has some theory that total coverage is good for the health). It is typical of Howard that he should assume a freshly prepared jacuzzi to be there for him to appropriate.

Not surprisingly, the first item on the agenda for the next management meeting was:

BATHROOM

Amelia and Barbara gave Howard a hard time for his cuckoo-like approach to others' filled baths and then, as so often, moved off the agenda for some impromptu Howard-baiting, this time on the subject of his smoking.

'The whole place smells like a public hice at claysing time,' said Amelia. 'If you can't restrain yourself, I'll have to start declaring no-smoking areas.'

I thought only judges used the phrase 'public house', but then Amelia's accent is likewise seldom heard beyond the senior judiciary. I'm against restrictions on liberty unless other things are very unequal, but paternalism moves me to support the campaign against Howard's smoking, for his lungs crackle with accumulated gunge and you can hear his every breath. Bunny chipped in poignantly, to urge him not to let himself get into her condition. The wretched state of her lungs is undeserved, for Bunny never even tried a fag when she was a schoolgirl.

'You'd do well to restrain yourself in certain other areas as well,' Barbara said.

Howard, who had so far endured the assaults in equable silence, replied, 'What's that supposed to mean?'

'I think you know what I'm referring to.' Barbara's baritone was ominously rich.

Howard affected his look of innocent bafflement.

'Let's just say,' continued Barbara, 'that advantage shouldn't be taken of young visitors.'

So she *had* heard the pig-sticking noise when Howard had romantically detained Nikki. Howard glared at Barbara, but said nothing. Usually he doesn't turn the other cheek to her for long, but he must have recognised that engaging her on this point would thrust the incident under the nose of Amelia, who could well regard it as grounds for eviction.

To avoid our straying further into that mine-ridden territory, I said, 'Can we please get back to the agenda. Have we finished with the bathroom?'

Regrettably the answer was no, as Amelia had views to express on the length of time Dennis spends there. 'We all know that you have a bit of a prublim in the prostate department, Dennis dear,' she said in her saccharine tone, 'but if you need a long, slow, ahem, piddle, there *are* alternatives to the main bathroom. There's the little one, and the loo downstairs.' She tittered and Dennis looked mortified. Then she continued, 'But I'm afraid the garden *isn't* an alternative. Mr Shanks takes rather a dim view of people going on his compost heap.'

Dennis added a blush to his look of mortification. I intervened: 'It seems to me, from what you report, that Mr Shanks's views are generally rather dim. If he brightened them up a bit, it would benefit himself and others. I'd have thought a drop of pee on the compost was just the job.'

'It *was* a drop,' said Dennis ruefully.

'Well, I'm sorry,' Amelia said more crisply, 'but the garden isn't a farmyard or a public convenience.' 'Public convenience' was from the same stable as 'public house'.

From the look on Barbara's face it was clear that, having been thwarted in her attempt to reveal Howard's seduction of Nikki, she was waiting for an opportunity to make trouble. She now growled: 'And neither the garden nor the house should be used for the other thing that men's lavatories are sometimes used for.'

She turned to Dennis with a look of fire. He isn't usually the butt of her attacks. Dennis returned a perplexed smile. The fiery glare continuing, he said, 'I hope you're not suggesting I do big-jobs on the compost heap.'

It's mildly depressing, the way these infantile phrases persist into, or resurface in, old age.

'You know that's not what I mean.' This was the technique

she had unavailingly tried on Howard. It was no more effective this time.

'I'm sorry, Barbara, but I haven't the faintest clue what you're talking about.'

'It may not be illegal any more, but it's still disgusting.'

'Filthy brown-hatters,' Joy interjected, speaking to no-one in particular.

There was a painful silence. Dennis blushed again, this time more deeply: his face was the colour of Howard's after fartlek. To my dismay I blushed too – because, I think, my half-formed private thoughts about Dennis had suddenly become starkly public. It was as if my own secret had been betrayed.

Barbara was quick to notice my blush and included me in her basilisk's gaze. 'Ha! Oscar and Bosie.'

'Mattress-munchers!' cried Joy. Where does she find these expressions?

'Shut up, Joy,' rapped Dennis, who had now regained some composure. 'Can we get this straight,' he said slowly and firmly to Barbara. 'Are you accusing me, and possibly others in this room, of – of unnatural practices?'

Dennis, when fully engaged, can be imposing. It was not for nothing that he was head of M&A at a firm of City solicitors.

Barbara, perhaps recognising that she had gone too far this time, looked rattled. 'I'm not saying anything,' she self-refutingly said. 'I'm just offering a piece of advice between friends.'

'And I'll offer you a piece of legal advice: innuendo is a form of defamation, and damages in defamation can bankrupt the defendant.'

'I hope we don't need to descend into legalese.'

'I expect an apology from you, *now*. Otherwise cordial relations between us are at an end.'

Although it isn't in Barbara's character to let herself lose face, she was on the verge of backing down when Howard – smarting from her allusion to his slap and tickle with Nikki – ruined everything by interjecting, 'Talk about pots and kettles! If these two are Oscar and Bosie, you and Amelia are Virginia and Vita, only without the literary flair.'

Barbara exploded. 'How dare you! How DARE you!'

Roland, who had been enjoying himself, said, 'Methinks the lady –'

'Shut up!' Barbara roared at him. 'Shut up!' Her outrage swept the room like the beam of a lighthouse, moving round to Howard again: 'How dare you!' Then it swept on to Amelia, who had no idea what anyone was on about. 'I'm not going to put up with gross insults from that vat of lard. Either he leaves the house or I do.' Whereupon she thudded from the room on her hideous bare feet and the meeting broke up in disarray.

I went to my room and shut the door, sick of the lot of them. We had formed the commune to console each other in the face of the awful and ineluctable facts of old age. Soon we'd all be dead: surely we could strive to be cheerful, or at least resigned, and to be kind to each other in the short time that remained? Instead, every time we got together there was spiteful bickering that would dishonour the playground of a nursery school. I asked myself whether I wouldn't be happier living alone, hard-up as I am, or even moving into an old people's home, where I would simply be looked after and could decide how much, if at all, I wanted to interact with the other inmates.

Pondering these thoughts, I was even less than usually pleased when Howard bumbled in. He was shaken by the way the meeting had ended, he was frightened of being turned out, and he rhetorically asked me where he would go and what he would do without his old friends. I was about to tell him coolly that he had brought all this on himself by his incontinent carrying-on with Nikki and his ill-advised accusation of Barbara and Amelia, when a tear rolled out of each of his eyes and mingled with the beads of sweat on his cheeks; so I suggested more emolliently that it would all blow over. Actually I doubted this; having narrowly avoided one eviction-grounding charge, he had exposed himself to another. My kindish words opened the sluices of his self-pity and he started to sob loudly, throwing himself at me and hugging me. There was a smell of alcohol, stale cigars and infested tweed. Between the sobs he gasped that he was just a useless fat old gubbins who exasperated everybody and might as well drop dead. I was inclined to agree.

Chapter 13

•

Last weekend Julian and Jemima Wormald, old friends of Bernard and Amelia, dropped in on their way to the Suffolk coast, where they are spending Christmas and New Year with the family. I inwardly wished them luck, for in my experience a trip to East Anglia in winter always results in bronchitis or worse: the icy wind is supposed to blow straight across from the Urals, whatever and wherever they are. Julian, who goes back years with Dennis and Bernard in the City, has a Roman nose that points sideways, giving a twang to his voice, which is a sonorous basso profundo: what with the effect of the nose, he sounds like Chaliapin played through an ancient phonograph. I believe that the Wormalds have a Jack Russell, and the image flitted through my mind of this dog looking into the horn as Julian's voice thundered out. Jemima is soft in manner but granitic in her political views, which she expresses in the archaic RP used by presenters of children's programmes in the early days of the BBC: Are you sitting comfortably? Then I'll begin: sex offenders should be castrated without anaesthetic; if they offend again, they should be put to death. She was launching into a philippic against the welfare state when Julian turned the conversation to the absence of Bernard.

'*So* sorry to have missed Bernie,' he boomed like a didgeridoo played in a tunnel. 'Damn shame. Where is the old scoundrel?'

Amelia had obviously been preparing for this question,

for her reply came out mechanically and too quickly. 'He's gone golfing with Biffy.'

'*Golfing*? At this time of year? Where?'

'Aldeburgh.'

I shuddered. Why on earth had we left it to Amelia to decide on the alibi without consultation – especially after the near disaster when Sarah and Angus had come to stay? It is true that the Wormalds had given little warning of their visit, but it was culpable laziness for us to treat that as an excuse for not meeting to agree on the line that Amelia should take. Amelia, after all, had found time to rehearse, even if she had put it to poor use.

His Master's Voice resounded again. 'But the Aldeburgh golf course –'

'Aldeburgh! That's just down the coast from Christopher and Sharon's,' tinkled Jemima, for whom it must be a trial to have a daughter-in-law called Sharon. 'We'll drop in on him.' The Wormalds, like King Lear, enjoy dropping in.

Julian: 'He'll be at the Wentworth, I suppose?'

Amelia, a rabbit in headlights, faintly replied, 'Oh – yes.'

Glances were traded at high volume among the communards. It crossed my mind that Amelia might, possibly under the influence of Barbara, have lost heart in the plot and be deliberately or recklessly undermining it: in that case the cadre was reduced to Roland, Bunny, Howard and me – i.e. we were doomed. Contrary to our agreed rule of leaving the talking to Amelia, I intervened to try to change the alibi. Playing for time while I tried to think something up, I said, 'I don't think Bernard said Aldeburgh, Amelia. It was somewhere quite different.'

Amelia looked at me as if she were the Queen Mother and I were the flunkey who was late in bringing her third G and T. 'He said Aldeburgh, dear. I ought to know. Golfing.' Her head titubated scattily.

If she wasn't deliberately undermining the plot, she was hysterically revelling in disaster or playing some game that I couldn't fathom – or she was too stupid to realise the effect of her words. Clearly there was no hope of changing the alibi, so we now have to find a way of defusing the time-bomb she has set ticking. Julian and Jemima have promised to Drop In on the way back from their holiday, so by then we shall need a convincing explanation why they will have found no sign of Bernard playing unseasonable golf on the Suffolk coast.

Chapter 14

•

Dr Pee has now received the consultant's report on Joy and the news is bad: the lump was removed from her rectum, but the cancer has spread, she is terminally ill and – another dire euphemism – palliative care has been proposed. Dennis, who oscillates between hollow bravery and bouts of tears, asked Pee how long Joy had to live, and Pee said that it could be weeks, months or longer, which doesn't rule out much. The next question was whether Joy should be told: Dennis was against it, on the ground that she was too confused to deal with the information, but Pee said that it was a condition of having Macmillan nurses that the patient be told of her condition. Barbara, having learnt this, said to Amelia in a loud voice that we couldn't have the house full of nurses, that Joy should therefore go into a hospice and that it was a merciful release for all concerned.

Pee agreed to visit The Graylings to break the news to Joy. Dennis, unsure that he was strong enough to cope on his own, asked me to be present. I was interested to see how Pee would proceed, for his bedside manner is notoriously brusque, a manner he may assume in order to discourage hypochondria. 'What do you expect at your age?' is a refrain of his.

The four of us gathered in the drawing-room. Pee began by saying, 'Joy, do you remember you were in hospital recently?' His tone was dull and cold. I thought of Barbara interrogating her on the landing.

Joy looked around uncertainly at Dennis and me, and Dennis nodded to her. On this cue she replied, 'Yes, vaguely.' She was even more beautiful than usual today. It occurred to me for the first time that she looked like Virginia Woolf: perhaps the thought was prompted by Howard's inflammatory mention of Virginia and Vita.

'And do you know why you were there?'

Joy again looked uncertainly around. Her expression had become doleful.

'You had a little operation, didn't you, my love,' Dennis prompted.

'Not really,' she said, hedging her bets.

'They removed a lump from your rectum,' said Pee.

'Disgusting!'

'The lump's gone, but cellular abnormalities were found elsewhere.'

'Cellular abnormalities' failed, as any fool could have foreseen, to penetrate the cloud in Joy's head. Joy replied, 'You talk too much. I want to go to sleep.'

'This is important, Joy. Do you understand what I'm saying?'

'I don't want to hear any more. It's time for my sleep.'

'Yes, you're right. But have you understood what I have told you?'

To put paid to further questions, Joy said, 'Yes, yes, of course I have. Now will you clear off? I want to go to sleep. Goodnight.' It was the middle of the afternoon.

'It means you're not really going to get better,' said Pee.

Dennis started to cry silently. On each side of his spectacles a tear hung like a stalactite.

'You're a slitty-eyed rascal,' Joy rejoined.

Discomfited, Pee lamely said, 'OK.' He clearly didn't know what to say or do next.

'I think,' I said, 'we've probably got as far as we're going to get.'

Pee seized on this intervention as an excuse to clear off, as Joy had urged.

The news about her cast a shadow over Christmas Day, when we were joined by Peggy, the philosopher befriended by Howard at the Over-Sixties. Her visit caused embarrassment, as Howard has been in disgrace since the uproar at the last management meeting. Contrary to his fear, and mine, he has not been ordered to leave, but Amelia and Barbara have sent him to Coventry, their intention apparently being to make him feel so uncomfortable that he'll go of his own accord. At the time of the meeting Amelia failed to grasp the topic of contention – partly because she is deaf, partly because she is too genteel to imagine that homosexuality (if she knows what it is) could ever be aired in conversation – but it's clear that afterwards Barbara enlightened her enough to turn her into an enemy of Howard.

Any friend of Howard is therefore apt to feel the icy wind that blows on him. This was hard on Peggy, who is affable enough in a hockey sticks sort of way although apt to turn rigorous without warning: I ventured some bland and unconsidered remark about the Stoics, and Peggy demanded to know whether I was referring to the early or middle Stoa. I lamely said that my observation was intended to apply to Stoicism generally. 'In that case, it's simply silly,' she replied. Peggy is rather masculine to be Howard's type and likes to refer to people as 'chaps': this word she extended to animals when, over sherry before Christmas lunch, the conversation moved to the question of their mental life. 'Of course old Descartes thought that chaps like these' – she gestured at Moth and Jeeves, who were observing an uneasy truce for the festive season – 'were just complex machines. He'd nail them to a board and start vivisecting them. He treated their screams as merely mechanical effects.'

Amelia shuddered and Roland laughed in a know-it-all manner. He then told Peggy, à propos of nothing, that he was going to appear on *Private Passions* and drew her into a discussion of Schopenhauer's influence on Wagner, and particularly of the question whether Wagner's Hans Sachs could be regarded as a Schopenhauerian figure. Roland trowelled on the charm and sparkled ostentatiously, first because he wanted to cover the traces of his misplaced condescension when they had met previously, second because this was a way of needling Bunny, who couldn't add to such a conversation, and third because he seemed genuinely to like Peggy. By the time we were on to our third sherry (lunch was delayed because, two hours after the turkey had gone into the oven, a smell of burning plastic revealed to Segunda that she had left in its breast the bag of giblets: it took some time to scrape away the melted plastic and to replace it with the stuffing that she had left forgotten on the draining-board) the exchange between Roland and Peggy had become flirtatious, and both Bunny and Howard were looking sour.

At 2.30 the gong sounded and we swayed into the dining-room. Amelia went to her usual place at the head of the table, where she has a little bell which she rings like an aged fairy to summon Segunda. Amelia had put on a festive dress of rustling blue satin which, during drinks, had worked its way so far between her buttocks that she had to yank it out with a hard tug before sitting down.

It was quickly apparent that the table was short of two covers, so the rest of us hung around looking uncomfortable. 'Segunda, dear,' said Bunny, 'we need another couple of places.'

'Mrs Bankes essay Ch'oward not ch'ere for lunch and nobody essay nothin about we ch'ave vista.'

Segunda had clearly been misled or suborned in a plot to humiliate Howard in front of his guest. Amelia smiled dreamily and Barbara glowered at Howard (a useful rhyme for the next time we do limericks). Barbara was wearing a red velvet smoking jacket and black trousers with a satin stripe down the side. I had to admit, to myself, that she looked rather dashing.

Bunny pressed on. 'Well there's obviously been a misunderstanding. Be a dear and lay another couple of places.'

Segunda frowned and busied herself with the carving of the turkey. There was a stand-off until Bunny, to avoid a scene, fetched the things herself. Segunda may have been under orders from Amelia, or it may simply have been that she was in no mood to accept instructions from Bunny, for Bunny had recently offended her by interfering in the cleaning. As a result of a lecture by a health expert to the Over-Sixties, Howard is currently on a jag of clean living and something called 'well-being' (neither of which, it seems, precludes drinking and smoking to excess). He reported to Bunny, in one of their tête-à-têtes, that the expert had said that the average household was awash with causes of cancer: one example is coloured lavatory paper (Howard speculated that it may have caused the disease in Joy), cling film is worse, and worse still are the materials we use to clean ourselves and our homes. Bunny, who is easily impressed by that sort of stuff, took it upon herself to expel from The Graylings all the carcinogenic things she could find. Our stock of super-soft bog paper – the sort that has on its packaging the drivel about puppies – has been replaced by something that looks and feels like sandpaper and that caused me to bleed after a vigorous wipe: I have not felt so much discomfort in that department since the heyday of Izal Medicated. The fluoride toothpaste has been replaced by a cement-like substance called Daffodil, which appropriately has caused those teeth that remain among us to go even yellower. Segunda's Mr Muscle and other favourites have been replaced by insipid fluids with no detectable cleansing properties: the laundry has gone radically non-biological and our underwear is going grey. When Amelia complained about this to Segunda, the latter was justly vexed to be blamed for a policy change that Bunny had thrust upon her.

After lunch we had presents. Bunny is a keen knitter – or, as Roland finds it funny to say, a prize knit – and gave us each a specially made garment. When, at the end of the summer, she announced that she was going to do this and asked us what we would like, we all pleaded with her not to go to the trouble, for her enthusiasm outruns her skill.

Roland pays for his snideness by receiving a series of jerseys that hang limply off him like suits of mail: he loses them as quickly as he can, but Bunny always has a new one ready. The chain-mail effect becomes more prominent with each new jersey, for, although Roland is shrinking from bone disease, Bunny knits the same size. I was given a woolly hat, generously deep in the style of Noddy: if I had unrolled it fully, it would have reached below my chin. Dennis got a Balaclava helmet and, when he peered through the chink, looked like the Yorkshire Ripper. Bunny's most ambitious effort was a pullover which was destined for a great-nephew but had got into the pile of knitwear for us: on the front was Thomas the Tank Engine, who pulled a train of carriages that were meant to run round the child's torso. Something had gone wrong and the train was squashed up, as if in some terrible accident.

'We'd better ask The Fat Controller what happened,' Roland said, nodding at Howard.

'Perhaps it will look OK when it's on,' Peggy suggested.

Moth may have been partly to blame for the railway accident, for he had made off with the ball of wool when Bunny was at a particularly tricky point. (There were, as a result, predictably hot words between Bunny and Barbara.) We can only hope that next year he is more persistent.

The day ended in alarm. In the evening we heard a shout of distress from Amelia in the bathroom. My first thought was that Howard had again slipped into the jacuzzi, but he was sprawled semi-conscious the other side of the drawing-room, a glass of Scotch beside him, the remains of a Hamlet precariously perched between his lips. Its ash had dropped on to his chest. Barbara hurried upstairs to investigate and soon her shouts replaced Amelia's. Girding myself to see Amelia naked – a prospect little more enticing than Bunny's nakedness when she got wedged in the bath – I joined the second wave of rescuers and we arrived to see blood gushing from Amelia's leg, which was propped on the bridge for soaps, sponges, etc. that straddled the bath. Amelia was lying in the water, which had gone brown from the mixture of blood and some green foam that Bunny had neglected to confiscate, or that Amelia had hidden in her bedroom. She looked like Marat assassinated. Barbara, good in an emergency, was tying a towel tightly below the knee of the bleeding leg.

'No men in here,' she barked. 'One of you phone an ambulance. Her varicose veins have burst.'

I was happy to run off and do this, for blood makes me queasy at the best of times. The view of exploded veins was too much on a stomach still full of Christmas pudding, and I had also seen more than I wanted of the remains of Amelia's cleavage.

Chapter 15

•

The day after Boxing Day Amelia was released from hospital with a bandage round her calf, and she now walks, at a more than usually dignified pace, with a stick that belonged to Bernard: it isn't suited to the lame, for it has a sword inside and a silver pummel, but Amelia scorned the aluminium crutch that the hospital offered. Awaiting her on her return was another envelope delivered by courier and addressed to Bernard: inside was a letter from the chairman of his old bank, Anthony Benton-Sadie, reporting on the meeting held to discuss the demand from Arnoldo & Miccolucci. All the surviving directors concerned had been present, along with Benton-Sadie and two lawyers from Dennis's old firm. The lawyers advised that the Italians didn't have a leg to stand on: it was therefore agreed unanimously that not an inch should be given and that the old directors would write defiant letters in identical terms. A letter for Bernard to sign was enclosed: once signed it was to be returned to the chairman who would dispatch all the letters together to Arnoldo & Miccolucci.

Amelia, having shown me the chairman's letter and the one for Bernard, confessed that there was a passage in the former that, as she put it, caused her a little unease:

> Given the suspected criminal backing of Arnoldo & Miccolucci, we cannot exclude the possibility that they will try to use illegal means of persuasion

where legal means fail. Although this risk should not be overestimated, the retired directors may wish to consider whether any precautions are appropriate. Such precautions must be a matter for the individuals concerned, as regrettably the Bank cannot assist in this respect.

'A little unease' would have been understatement in the mouth of anyone with nerves less steely than Amelia's. The chairman's words certainly rattled me.

'Some dreadful little Sicilian with a five o'clock shadow is going to turn up with a violin case, pull out a machine-gun and mow us all down,' Amelia said airily. 'It's too awful, darling.' While she was talking, she scrawled Bernard's signature as swiftly as she would have done her own: the speed and accuracy of the forgery were, as estate agents say, stunning.

I again tentatively raised the possibility of her informing the Italians that Bernard was dead: it could imperil our project of giving everyone else, and Sarah in particular, to believe that Bernard was still alive; but that peril looked less oppressive than the one of being mown down by bullets. Arnoldo & Miccolucci would probably concentrate their efforts on the surviving directors. Even if they went after the estate, it would be Sarah's problem, not Amelia's.

'So you think I should leave my own daughter to the mercies of the Mayfia,' Amelia replied. 'She is a pill, it's true, but a mother has...' She trailed off abstractedly, as she so often does, and appeared to be turning over in her mind the idea of directing the man with the violin case towards

Sarah. From the smile playing around the corners of Amelia's lips, the idea seemed to have its charms. She pulled herself together. 'No, my dear, we have good reason to keep Bernard alive. We can't be put off our stride by a couple of foreigners with silly names. If Bernard is dead, Sarah will have us out of The Graylings on our ear. That's the reason we started this scheme, wasn't it? We'll just have to hope the Sicilian can't find us. The turning on to the drive is easy to miss. Don't mention any of this to the others: don't want to frighten the horses, do we?' She picked up the sword-stick and started limping majestically from the room.

'Tis the season of A and E. The following day, and thus only three days after Amelia's veins burst, Jeeves was rushed to the vet. He had been asleep on the sofa, and Howard, absently mistaking him for a cushion, sat on him, breaking three of his ribs. The mistake was excusable, for Jeeves is so shaggy that you can't discern his legs or easily make out which end of him is which. The seriousness of the injury was due in part to Howard's method of sitting down: instead of bending his legs and easing himself on to the seat as any other Christian would, he simply lets himself fall over backwards, landing with great momentum. He has already broken one of Amelia's Georgian dining-chairs in this way and he cracked another by leaning back and tipping it on to its hind legs. He does this mainly when laughing. At a lunch when he was next to me, he hooted at something, tipped back too far and grabbed me to restore his balance; but I too was naughtily tipping, so we both went over backwards, Howard in the process kicking the under-side of the table, which caused a bottle of wine to fall over.

Once we and it had been righted and the mess cleared up, Amelia forbade him to laugh at table again.

It is fortunate that the sofa is yielding, or that would have been the end of Jeeves. Bunny, recognising his shriek as a mother would her baby's cry, came puffing into the drawing-room as quickly as her ailments would let her and discharged a battery of abuse at Howard. Then, instead of going to Jeeves's aid, she subsided into a chair, put her elbows on her knees and her face in her hands and sobbed abundantly. Jeeves remained on the sofa, squashed, immobile, whimpering and unattended until Barbara entered and – nobly, for she sides with Moth in the feud of the four-legged – went to make him as comfortable as she could. She then picked up where Bunny had left off in the tirade against Howard. It was the first time Barbara had uttered a word to him since the management meeting, but in the circumstances this could not be viewed as a thaw.

Bunny is usually ready to find the bright side of disasters, so her melodramatic reaction was a surprise. My suspicion that it was partly caused by something other than the crushing of Jeeves was confirmed the next day when, in a break from a struggle with the relation between reliance and contractual obligation, I walked past the door of the drawing-room on my way to make a coffee. Bunny and Howard were sitting close to each other, talking quietly, on the sofa where the crushing had occurred. It was mid-afternoon and no-one else was about. As I passed the door, he made to put his arm round her, and she withdrew, edging further down the sofa. I moved away from the door and, being human, hung around to listen.

'Don't. I think you've done enough damage.' Bunny sounded tense and angry.

'I've told you I'm sorry. I'm a great clumsy ass, I know. I didn't sit on the dog on purpose. And it's going to be fine.'

'It's not that, you fool. It's not just that. It's just all too much. It's too much.'

There was a silence. I looked over my shoulder to check that I was not being watched by a second-order spy.

Then Howard said, 'What's too much for what?'

'The way you carry on. The way you've always carried on. You've never had any respect for me.'

'I've loved you for decades. I still do. You know I do.'

'I don't think so. I've just been a comfort blanket for when a wife or some other bit on the side had had enough of you.'

'I've never thought of you as a bit on the side.'

'It's what I've been, though, whatever you told yourself. When it came to a commitment, when I got pregnant –' There was another silence. 'You'd forgotten all about it.'

'You know it wasn't possible.'

'No? You found it possible with enough other women. It was my last chance: I was 43.'

'Roland would have –'

'You don't think Roland was going to oblige – we hadn't slept together for 20 years.' Another silence. 'Neither of you ever loved me. I've been a scullery maid to him and a tart to you. And now you're at a loose end, it suits you to try it on again.'

You think you know your old – nay, ancient – friends intimately, and then you are faced with a great vista which you never dreamt of. Tiptoeing on to the kitchen, I wondered how much, if anything, Roland knew of all this.

Chapter 16

•

Dennis told Dr Pee that he would like to hear directly from the consultant about Joy's condition and prospects, so Pee gave him a phone number. But the consultant was guarded by a fiery griffin of a secretary, who referred Dennis to a registrar, one Dr Zayat. Dennis only now realised the fact, known to most, that the NHS is staffed almost entirely by foreigners. Zayat told Dennis on the phone that he couldn't remember the case but that he would check his records and phone back. The next morning Dennis found the following message on his phone:

'Mr Middleton, Dr Zayat here. I've now checked the case of your late wife. She had a moderate tumour in the rectum, which was successfully removed. It certainly wouldn't have been the cause of her death. A heart attack is the likely explanation. Cheers.'

Dennis is understandably perplexed. On the one hand he and Joy have been told that Joy is dying of cancer; on the other, the latest information is that she is already dead, but not from cancer. Taking into account the visitor who appeared on the doorstep while Joy was in hospital, there seems to be a swelling desire among the staff there to write her off, but she's still kicking, as we all see daily. Dennis suspects another confusion of identity. His pursuit of the facts continues.

So does his pursuit of Oik, who has started giving him lifts into the village, and further afield, on the back of the motorbike. Dennis's arthritis makes it hard for him to get or stay on, and we have all used this and other reasons to try to persuade him not to be Oik's passenger; but he replies that we are a lot of fuddy-duddies and that if he doesn't have fun now he won't get another chance. He looks rather butch in Oik's spare crash-helmet, which says 'Ongar Blue Angels'. I can't fathom the relation between those two. The apparently genuine surprise with which Dennis greeted Barbara's accusation at the management meeting suggests, but doesn't prove, that he is free of fruity inclinations: perhaps he just misses the company of young people, takes a fatherly interest and hopes to do good to a misfit. But in that case why did he emerge from Oik's shed yesterday with a black eye and a red mark on his neck? It was pretty obvious that Oik had grabbed him by the throat and biffed him, but then why had he done that? Two plausible hypotheses are (1) that Dennis had made a pass which Oik had beaten off and (2) that they both enjoy a bit of rough. Doubt is cast on (2) by Oik's vigorous shagging of Segunda, but he may be versatile. When we asked Dennis what had happened, he was irritable and uncommunicative, saying only that it was a little accident which he didn't want to discuss.

Chapter 17

•

In the autumn we managed to get through the annual visit of Sarah and Angus without exciting any serious degree of suspicion about Bernard's absence: Sarah did ask whether there was anything wrong – a question that inspired Bunny's cretinous 'was' remark; but Howard's inspired attack of cramp deflected the conversation, and the rest of the visit passed without incident. As we waved goodbye to Sarah and Angus, we heaved a sigh of relief at the thought that we were free for another year from the burden of entertaining them with alibis, for they don't bother to keep in touch between visits.

The sigh was premature, for last week Sarah turned up out of the blue. That was bad enough, but the news she had for us was worse: Angus is being transferred to the bank's head office this spring, so they will be moving back to London. 'We'll be able to visit you much more often,' Sarah said with forced brightness, and Amelia politely replied with no greater conviction. The rest of us grinned weakly. Lying once a year to someone who lives on the other side of the Atlantic is one thing: it's quite another to keep her off the scent when she lives less than an hour away and makes frequent visits – some of them probably unannounced, like this one. Had we known this was in prospect, we surely never would have entered into the plot to conceal Bernard's death.

Sarah is over to hunt for a flat, or an apartment as she has come, since her semi-Americanisation, to call it. 'It's likely to take me a few weeks to find something,' she told us. 'The bank has put me up at the Waldorf, but it will do me good to come down here for a weekend or two.' This was something for us all to look forward to.

Inevitably the question of the missing Bernard came up. 'I can't believe this. Dad and I are the little man and the little lady on the barometer: whenever I come in, he goes out.' We all went ha ha ha. 'So, where is he this time?'

Amelia had had no time to prepare. My bowels loosened as I awaited her impromptu reply. Given that we had to keep up the pretence for several weeks, her best course would have been to play the 'he's gone on a cruise' card, but she had either forgotten it or decided to keep it up her sleeve for the time when Sarah and Angus moved to England for good. What she came up with was: 'He's away on business an awful lot these days. They seem to have dragged him right out of retirement. He's in London at the mo, for some board meeting.'

Why does she always locate Bernard in the place to which the questioner is just about to go? She had told Julian and Jemima Wormald, who were on their way to the Suffolk coast, that Bernard was in Aldeburgh. The Wormalds haven't yet Dropped In on their way back, so we still have to dream up something to explain why they will have failed to find Bernard there. I'm appalled by the prospect that Amelia will give conflicting stories to the Wormalds and to Sarah and that they will then compare notes. Even if we manage to avoid a contradiction there, the web is bound to tangle sooner or later when Sarah and Angus are constantly around and talking to family friends. If and when that happens, we'll have to fall back on Amelia's well-attested vagueness, but how often can that excuse be made without losing its force?

Sarah was not letting the matter drop. 'So, will he be home tonight? Because I'll stay over if I may.'

'Oh no, darling.'

'Oh no what? He won't be back, or I can't stay?'

'Of course you can stay. No, I mean Daddy won't be back tonight.'

'Why not? It's only a commute: he used to do it twice a day. They've surely given him a chauffeur?'

Amelia's famous poise was showing signs of wear and tear. 'Oh look, I don't know. He said he'd be away a few days. Perhaps it wasn't London. Switzerland it might have been – Zürich.'

'Don't you two ever communicate?'

Amelia recovered herself and smiled regally. 'Your father and I are past the need for communication about that sort of thing.'

'So, your communication is at a deeper level only, like John Bayley and Iris Murdoch after she went potty? That must make the house easy to run. How does the maid know how many to cook for?'

I feared that Sarah might interrogate Segunda, but then reflected that it was unlikely, for Sarah is aloof with servants – another disagreeable habit she has picked up from the Americans, or a certain subset of them.

The next day she went into London to start her search for the flat, but she is back again this weekend and the third degree on the subject of Bernard has resumed. 'So,' Sarah said to her mother over lunch, 'you said he'd gone to Zürich on business. That was at the beginning of the week. You said he'd be away a few days. How long are they keeping him there? I thought he'd gone to a board meeting. How long can a board meeting last?'

Amelia was reduced to sighing, shrugging and dreamily smiling.

Sarah looked round at us over her half-moons with her icy blue eyes. 'I think you must have murdered him and hidden the corpse.' She displayed a wintry smile. Her efforts at humour are never successful – this being a striking case in point.

I felt myself blush. Howard had gone purple and shiny and the others were squirming, with the exception of Joy, who said to no-one in particular, 'Yes, they hid the corpse.'

'Joy, be a good girl,' Dennis said firmly.

'Sarah, what a horrible thing to say, even in jest!' said Barbara. Perhaps she is still toeing the line after all and her veiled threat, when she caught us talking about her, was just a tantrum.

Sarah was not cowed. 'Nikki told me there was a new mound in the pets' cemetery.'

'Sarah, *please*,' said Amelia. The general blushing and squirming increased.

'Well I want to speak to Dad. You've presumably got a contact number for him?'

'Oh God, I don't know. I'll have to look after lunch.'

'What about his mobile? You must know that number.'

'Mobile? I don't think he has one of those.'

'Rubbish. He's phoned me from it before now. Let me have the number. I'll call him after my walk, to see when he's coming back.'

Sarah, keen on fitness, takes a vigorous walk after every meal (she scorns our gym). Her walk after lunch gave us a little time to decide how to deal with the threatened call to the mobile, so we adjourned to the drawing-room for an emergency meeting. Concentration was an effort, for, unlike Sarah, the communards treat Saturday lunch as the prelude to a zizz, and our body clocks have adapted to the routine. Dennis and Joy, not being part of the plot, went up to their room and Howard, having settled into his chair, snored like a hog while the rest of us discussed what to do. We agreed that it was pointless for Amelia to maintain the fiction that she didn't know the number of Bernard's mobile: Sarah would soon find it somehow or look for other ways of getting in touch with her father. We also agreed that we should get the mobile and phone it to check whether it had an 'I can't take your call' message, either in Bernard's voice d'outre-tombe or in the honeyed tones of the Vodafone lady: depending on what it said, the message might help us or make things worse.

Contrary to her earlier representation, Amelia knew where to find the phone – it was on the desk in Bernard's study, as always – and brought it down to the drawing-room. She had also found the number, which she called from the land-line. The mobile started playing *Eine Kleine Nachtmusik* in synthetic beeps piercing enough to wake Howard. After five reprises we begged Amelia to hang up: there was clearly no recorded message.

'That's all right then,' said Roland. 'Sarah will phone and get no reply. She can't draw any conclusions from that. Most people don't leave their mobile on.'

'It's just postponing the problem,' Barbara replied. 'She'll try again. If she still can't get through, she'll try other means. Someone ought to answer, pretend to be Bernard and put her off the track.'

This struck me as too clever by half. Perhaps, despite the favourable signs over lunch, Barbara was after all trying to destroy the plot, by enticing us into self-betrayal through some high-risk gimmick. I voiced the 'too clever by half' portion of this thought, but the others thought it an excellent wheeze. They also voted that I should be the impersonator of Bernard, on the ground that my voice was the most similar to his.

'It may be the most similar,' I rejoined, but it's still not remotely like his voice. I'm blessed with a fluty tenor: Bernard had more of the baritone sax.' Having said this, I reflected that Barbara's voice was closer than mine to Bernard's, but I didn't have the nerve to say so. People who phone The Graylings and get Barbara think that they are talking to one of the male residents. When they get me they often say 'Hallo Bunny'.

'Yours is more oboey than fluty,' Howard cattily observed. 'And poor Bernard's got more baritone-saxy the more he drank and smoked.'

'Hardly for you to make comments like that, old boy, if I may say so,' said Roland. 'Your voice sounds like a harmonium with a nest of mice in the bellows, and for the same reason.'

Barbara: 'Can we *please* keep to the point. Sarah will be back from her walk before we know where we are.' She turned to me. 'If you're worried about your voice, talk in a whisper or something, and pretend you're in a meeting or have laryngitis.'

'I haven't said I'll do it.'

But the cries of 'go on', 'please', 'you must', etc. were rather gratifying, and anyway, if everyone was set on the idea, the only other potential impersonators (apart from Barbara) were Howard and Roland: they would be sure to bugger the thing up and put us in still greater danger. So, with a great show of reluctance, I agreed. The next question was what I should say. I mentioned the cruise gambit: this, combined with the meeting-in-Zürich opening, should do the trick. The script we came up with ran along these lines:

'Hallo, darling. Lovely to hear your voice. Delighted that you're both coming back to blighty. So sorry we keep missing each other: Mummy will have told you that I'm out here in Zürich, dabbling in some of the old money stuff again. And guess what? Old Stuffer's on the case as well.' (It's dispiriting that most of Bernard's friends have infantile nicknames. Stuffer is fictitious (it seemed safer), but Biffy is real enough, even though Amelia made up the golfing holiday. Other real members of Bernard's circle are Dandy, Minty and Cackles: the list continues.) 'You remember Stuffer? The one with the giant conk. He's here with his charming wife Beryl. They're going on after this for a cruise: it starts in the Med and goes to the Bahamas. They've suggested I come along too – said it would do my throat good. I keep getting this bloody laryngitis: you'll hear it in my voice, if you can hear me at all. Well, d'you know, I've said yes. Your mother will kill me – or perhaps she'll be glad not to have me under her feet, ha ha. So I'm afraid I won't see you when you're over this time – yet again. Never mind. Big kiss. Pip pip.'

We agreed that I should have a rehearsal: Amelia would call the mobile again and I would answer in my Bernard-with-laryngitis voice and run through the lines. But before we had a chance even to start, we heard Sarah's key in the front door. Amelia hurriedly handed me the phone. Had my presence of mind been full, I would have carried it at a leisurely pace up to my room at the top of the house, where I could take Sarah's call in safe privacy, but I confusedly de-cided that I couldn't let Sarah see me with the mobile, and to get to the staircase I would have had to pass her in the hall, so I darted into what is known as the parlour, a small and seldom used room adjoining the drawing-room: it's for people to write letters in and so forth – there's a supply of biros, paper and envelopes – but none of us is much of a correspondent, so the biros have gone dry and the paper yellow, the envelopes have lost their stick, and the radiator has been turned off, making the parlour as hostile to human habitation as the surface of Mars (or the saloon).

Having hurriedly shut the door behind me, I put my ear to it and heard Sarah come into the drawing-room. There was some desultory chat, then Amelia went out to make some tea, then she came back, then there was more chat, and then Sarah returned to the question of the mobile phone. My heart started beating furiously. Amelia an-nounced that she had found the number.

'I might as well try Dad now,' said Sarah. 'I'll phone him from here if you don't mind: it's so nice and warm by the fire.'

I now realised what a klutz I had been to rush into the parlour: apart from the cold, I would be no more than a few feet away from Sarah when we spoke. There was a door between us, true, and I would be croaking with faux-laryngitis, but there was still a risk that she would hear me through the door. There was no way out of the parlour other than through the drawing-room, a vicious rambling rose precluding exit through the window: I thought of making a dash for it, but before I could decide whether or not to do so the mobile started to squeal out *Eine Kleine Nachtmusik*. Christ, I had forgotten about the ringer. I squeezed the horrible thing to my breast and cowered with it over some cushions on the chaise-longue to muffle the noise, but this made it very difficult to answer. My anxiety made me sweat so much, despite the temperature, that the phone slithered in my hands and I dropped it on the floor. Finally I managed to answer.

'Hallo?' I rasped.

My own voice rasped back: 'Hallo?' There was an echo on the line: that was all I needed.

Then Sarah spoke. 'Hallo? Dad?'

I could hear her through the door as well as down the phone. In that case she might hear me through the door, just as I had feared.

'Sarah, how lovely! Sorry, I've got the most awful throat: can you hear me all right?'

'You don't sound yourself at all. What are you taking for it?'

The conversation got going, I relaxed into the part, and everything went swimmingly till she asked me which hotel in Zürich I was staying in. Frequenting the world of finance, she would know all the hotels, but I have never been to Zürich in my life. Bernard would stay only in the grandest place: I seemed to remember that there was a smart hotel called the Baur au Lac and another one called the Goldener Hirsch, and that one was in Zürich and the other in Salzburg, but I couldn't recall which was which. If I had been calm, the Lac would have given me a clue, but I recklessly said 'The Goldener Hirsch'.

'The Goldener Hirsch? I didn't know there was one in Zürich. Is it new?'

'A chain now, I suppose. They all are.'

'Give me the number in case I get the chance to call you again. It's cheaper than ringing the mobile.'

'Er, I've no idea what the number is, darling.'

'Don't worry, I can find it on the net. What's your room number?'

I started to stutter and burble.

'Wait a minute,' Sarah said. 'I haven't got a pen.'

The next thing I knew, the door from the drawing-room burst open and Sarah strode in. Holding the mobile in full view, I gawped at her in terror from the corner of the chaise-longue. She was startled to see me.

'Oh, excuse me: I didn't know there was anyone in here. I was just getting something to write with.'

She went over to the escritoire and helped herself to one of the dried-up biros from the jar. She tried scribbling with it on the blotter, it didn't work, of course, so she tried another, repeating the process till she found one with ink that was only viscous rather than solid. As I was clearly supposed to be in the middle of some other phone call, the fiction required that I continue it, so I said down the mobile, 'Well, as you know, I have never asserted that you could catch all forms of joint action with a single model.' Realising with horror that I was still using my Bernard-with-a-sore-throat voice, I switched to the normal fluty, or oboey, tenor: 'No... But if that were right, you'd be unable to sustain a distinction between, say, agreements and concerted practices under Article 101... Exactly...'

I was rather pleased with my ability to imitate one side of a conversation: perhaps I should have gone on the boards (not Bernard's sort) instead of into legal theory. The money would not have been any worse, and as an undergraduate I was quite a hit on stage. My Old Gobbo was admired. Several of my companions in university am dram went on to become professionals: most never made it beyond the back legs of a stage cow in seaside rep, but a couple became household names – a fact I resent, for their acting was no better than mine. Then again, Domestos is a household name.

I managed to keep this up till Sarah had returned to the drawing-room. As she walked out, she gazed at me severely over her half-moons, her Cambridge-blue eyes narrowed and at their steeliest. Then her voice came back down the phone: 'Sorry, Dad, I had to go into the parlour. You should throw out those pens – they are prehistoric.'

The double-voice effect was now more noticeable, the voice that came through the door being much louder. Sarah had not shut the door properly and it had swung open: she was sitting just the other side of the doorway and we were staring straight at each other.

'So, what's your room number?' she asked again.

As softly as I could, I muttered, 'Ah, ah, you know – I don't know.'

'Dad, you'll have to try and speak up: I can't hear. Are you in your room now?'

'Yes.'

'Well, open your door, can't you, and see what the number is on it.'

'The door's already open,' I whispered, 'as you can see.'

We were still eyeballing each other. What the hell was I saying? Pulling myself together, I grasped that she had given me a lucky break: in the time she expected Bernard to open his door and look at the number, I could get up and close the door between parlour and drawing-room. This manoeuvre I executed. The strain was telling on me now: there were droplets of sweat on my upper lip and my vest was sticking to my back: bronchitis, with double doses of what Segunda calls 'Lem-Sick', is a dead cert.

The screws tightened when we moved on to the cruise. Sarah, shocked by the proposal, and specifically by the affront to Amelia implied by 'my' intention to leave her behind, pressed me with all sorts of questions that put me in corners. Which port did the cruise start from? What was the name of the ship? What line was it? Not the man to ask about cruise lines, I fobbed her off as best I could with 'I don't know', 'Stuffer and Beryl have the details' and vagueness.

'Have you even told Mum about this yet?' she asked accusingly.

'No, my dear: I've only just been invited. I was planning to phone your mother this evening.'

'Well you can jolly well tell her now: she's sitting right here.'

It was a relief to get Sarah off the phone, but pursuing the conversation with Amelia caused the new problem that I would have to pipe up to overcome her deafness, thereby increasing the risk that Sarah would hear me through the door, especially as her ear was no longer to the receiver. I reflected that it might be an emotional trial for Amelia to pretend to be talking to her recently dead husband, but she put on a sporting show, frigidly claiming not to mind at all that she was being left to sit out the dead part of the winter in Essex while Bernard and his cronies swanned round the equator. 'Don't overexcite yourself at quoits with Buffer,' she concluded with verisimilar sarcasm, having misheard the made-up name. 'Bye then, dear. Send us a card.'

I switched off the mobile and collapsed back on the chaise-longue, feeling like Olivier after a performance of *Othello*. If acting took this sort of toll, perhaps I was better off not being a household name. I lay there till I started to shiver, then tottered into the drawing-room, where Sarah was sounding off about her father's je-m'en-foutisme. The others, who were trying to join in, furtively nodded and winked at me in congratulation as, with quivering hand, I seized a chocolate digestive.

With luck, we have now got Sarah off our backs, in re Bernard's absence, till the end of her current stay, but God knows how we are going to keep the story going when she and Angus come back to England for good. Maybe we can orchestrate a grand row between Sarah and Amelia (not difficult, given the precedents) that would result in the former's refusing ever to visit The Graylings again. Or maybe – taking Arnoldo & Miccolucci into account – we should make a clean breast of it, whatever the appalling consequences.

Chapter 18

•

The course on opera having come to an end, Amelia has signed up for Psychology and Therapy. This has various elements, including 'basic sexuality for men', 'a path through menopause' (each of these n/a to Amelia), 'stress in relationships', 'managing anger', 'our spiritual journey' and 'exploring dreams'. Amelia has plumped for stress in relationships. The first assignment for the students was to examine the relationships of the people at home and to consider how they might be improved. Amelia, although as deaf as a snake and as vague as a patch of mist, is not unperceptive and is therefore aware – an amoeba would be aware – that life at The Graylings is, as she put it, not completely harmonious. A more accurate representation would be to say that we are a case study from Laing, what with Barbara and Amelia herself having sent Howard to Coventry, the arctic relations between Barbara and Dennis, Dennis's exhausting devotion to a senile and possibly (who knows?) dying wife and his possibly (who can be sure?) homosexual pursuit of a juvenile delinquent, the loveless marriage of Roland and Bunny, the secret, passionate and resentment-laden tension between Bunny and Howard, and the darker secret, shared by all, of Bernard's hidden corpse.

However the situation is described, Amelia declared that her assignment could clear the air and she invited us to participate. The idea was that we would each complete a personality test and then get together to discuss the results, with Amelia as 'facilitator'. (There was no reason to expect her to be any more effective in this role than she is as chair, or difficilitator, of the management meetings.) In the light of the strengths and weaknesses that the tests revealed, we would discuss how we might change our practices so as to 'build our performance as a team'. I couldn't see why in the first place we were supposed to be a team, except in an uninterestingly attenuated sense: the word suggested that the course leader was recycling material from one of those idiotic programmes for business executives. A lot of resistance was expressed, ranging from embarrassment (Bunny: 'Oh dear, I hate to think what a personality test would say about me') through impatience (Dennis: 'I don't think we're going to get anywhere washing our dirty linen together') to contempt (Roland: 'It's a vapid women's-magazine parlour game'), but, as always, we were bored and so we decided to give it a go.

After breakfast Amelia handed out the test to all of us except Joy, who was put in front of the jigsaw of the firemen. It was multiple-choice and we were told to answer the questions quickly without thinking about them for too long. Roland said there was no risk of that in this house. The numerical results were then translated into points on graph paper and you joined up the points with a line. If you were a perfectly rounded personality, the line made a circle, but your shape was likely to be skewed or, as Amelia paradoxically put it, your circle would not be round. A skew towards the top left meant that you were intellectual/analytical; towards the bottom right, that you were warm/emotional; and so on: the more pronounced the skewing, the stronger the personality trait in question. Amelia's manual would then tell you which occupations best suited your shape.

Some of the results seemed to fit us quite well: Dennis's, for example, showed him to be quite warm/emotional, but his most pronounced skewing was towards the practical (top right): the manual advised him to go into human resources. Roland was the big surprise: his shape stretched far down towards the warm/emotional bottom right, and the manual advised him to become a social worker.

'That just shows how appearances can be deceptive,' said Amelia. 'Underneath that curmudgeonly old exterior, Roland's quite cuddly.' She giggled.

'The alternative conclusion is that the test is a lot of cock,' Roland replied. 'How should we decide between these hypotheses? If your granddaughter were here she'd no doubt tell you to pick the one that's true for you.'

Amelia was not going to be put off her stride. 'So, you see, we're all different personality types, and to work together as a team we need to play to our strengths. Dennis and Barbara, you're the practical ones, so you should organise us all.'

Dennis and Barbara were not glad to be lumped together. They smiled bitterly, neither looking at the other.

'And Bunny and Roland, you're the warm and emotional ones, so we should come to you with our problems.'

'What if we have problems with each other?' Roland asked drily. He and Bunny likewise didn't look at each other. Bunny emitted a short and tinny laugh.

Amelia now asked us to consider ways in which we could

improve the team's performance. The manual prompted her to invite suggestions for 'fun together'. All minds went blank except that of Howard, who proposed a musical evening, and we agreed (with various degrees of enthusiasm) to the plan, for most of us have played an instrument at some point in our lives. Howard used to be the trombonist in an amateur jazz band. He told me that he had chosen the trombone because as a child he had been excited by brass instruments and this was the easiest one to play: if you hit a wrong note you can slide up or down till you find the right one, feigning an intentional glissando. He still has a trombone and gives it an occasional blow but, as he said wistfully, it's not much fun playing by yourself. The blows used to take place in his room to the accompaniment of recorded big-band music, but when I made a fuss he started using the ghetto-blaster in the gym – not the perfect venue, as there was little room to move the slide between the fitness machines: he dented it against the weight-lifting frame and his glissandos are now saccadic. Last summer he tried a one-man jam in a nearby field, but the cows were startled and the farmer threatened to shoot him.

The most accomplished musician among us is Joy, who studied the piano at music college. She was not good enough for a solo career, and started having children, so she became one of those middle-class women of whom loyal friends and relations say, 'She might have been a concert pianist' in that thin sense of 'might'. Nowadays she won't take the initiative to play and she can't learn anything new, but if you sit her in front of the Bechstein she will, if in the mood, perform one of the pieces she has known for years. These include several numbers by Cole Porter, and it was decided that, to open the musical evening, we'd ask her to play some of these while Howard played the melody on the trombone. It worked quite well on the night: we had 'Night and Day', 'I Get a Kick Out of You' and 'Begin the Beguine', but Joy sometimes strayed into other pieces, including something dark by Scriabin. During these divagations, Howard manfully improvised where possible, but sometimes broke for a drink, à la George Melly, leaving the floor to Joy.

Next were some piano duets by Amelia and Bunny. There had been a dispute between them over the programme, Amelia – whose repertoire is the more refined – wanting Brahms, Bunny holding out for 'Boiled Beef and Carrots'. In the event both were included, but the performers were much less skilled than Joy and didn't play well as a 'team': Bunny liked to rattle along while Amelia strove for ritardandos, and twice they got so badly out of step that they had to stop and start again. By the end both were tetchy, despite the exaggerated applause from all but Joy, who said, 'Pitiful performance.'

Roland was too frightened of humiliation to volunteer to play, but we cajoled him into getting out his long-neglected bassoon. I can't understand why anyone invented this instrument, which sounds as if it had a blockage. Certainly it didn't get the chance to redeem itself in the hands and lips of Roland, who had a go at an easy bit from Mozart's concerto. His Parkinson's was bad, so his lips made the reed squeak and his shaky fingers kept missing the keys. Halfway through he gave up in fury and went to sulk at the far end of the room, whence he made snide remarks during Dennis's lusty but multiply inaccurate rendering of 'Won't You Come Home Bill Bailey'. Roland's commentary became so intrusive that Howard loudly went Shshshsh: Dennis took this to be directed at him, broke off his song and angrily demanded to know from Howard what was wrong.

Contrary to Amelia's team-building intention, the evening was petering out into the usual acrimony and re-crimination, but during the bickering Joy walked back to the piano and started an allemande from one of Bach's French suites. Her playing was luminous. We all fell silent. As she played, she leant back and closed her eyes. Of the audience's eyes, several filled with tears as we pondered on the contrast between this performance and Joy's general mental condition, and on the possibility, given her equivocal death-sentence, that this was her swan-song.

Chapter 19

•

Perhaps because of the musical team-building exercise, but more probably because of the benign effluxion of time, Amelia and Barbara are saying the odd word again to Howard: relations are hardly amicable, but he is no longer in Coventry – perhaps Leamington Spa. His confidence thus boosted, Howard tried to infect us with enthusiasm for his latest fad, the drinking of one's own urine, which he claimed provides one with valuable additional minerals. The hackneyed example of Gandhi was cited, reminding Roland of a joke whose punch line was that Gandhi was a super-calloused fragile mystic hexed by halitosis; but Roland couldn't remember the story that led to this. Howard told us that it was best to drink your first pee of the day, which has got nice and strong overnight, and he tried to reassure us that there was nothing disgusting about it as you diluted it so much that it couldn't be tasted – in which case, I pointed out, it didn't seem to make any difference whether the undiluted pee was especially strong.

Dennis said that he and Joy were having nothing to do with it, as his emictions were already fraught and hers too erratic to be incorporated in a dietary regime. (Recently, when a damp stain appeared under Joy while she was sitting in front of the jigsaw, Dennis lamely cried, 'Darling, do be careful, you've spilt some white wine,' as he hurried out for cloth and detergent. She had not been drinking any at the time. Fortunately neither Amelia nor Barbara was present.) The rest of us were prepared to try the pee-drinking. I would have been happy enough knocking it back in my own room, but Howard insisted on taking command of the project and asked us each to provide him with a sample, which he would take into the kitchen before breakfast and dilute to the degree prescribed in his book on well-being: it would then be presented at table in the glasses that usually contain orange juice.

On the first morning we glanced uneasily at the glasses, the liquids in which were tinted various shades of yellow. Segunda, as she brought in the sausages, was stony-faced and in clattering mood, presumably as a result of having had to negotiate her way around Howard and six samples of piss in the kitchen. Grimacing in anticipation, we raised the glasses to our lips. I found it hard to bring myself to swallow and was unsure whether I could taste the pee or was just imagining it.

'How do you know you're drinking your own stuff and not someone else's?' mused Dennis from his position of comfortable detachment.

We all stopped drinking. Barbara spat her mouthful into a teacup. Then we put our glasses slowly down on the table, eyeing them this time with horror rather than unease. We turned to Howard.

'Don't worry,' he said breezily. 'I'm pretty sure I gave each person the right one.'

'*Pretty* sure?' I said.

'Well, it won't matter if you do have somebody else's. In fact it will probably do you more good: you'll be getting some different minerals.'

'You're missing out something important,' said Roland. 'Pee is like socks and farts: your own are OK, but other people's are disgusting.'

'I think I'll just have a little toast for breakfast,' said Amelia, who was looking grey.

And so the first morning of the regime was the last. Howard, undeterred, proposed that we replace urine with vinegar, which the well-being book recommended as an internal cleaner. We were prepared to go along with this, on the basis that there was nothing to mix up, and for a couple of weeks now have been starting breakfast with Sarson's instead of Tropicana. Praying that this, and nothing more sinister, was the reason for the stabbing pains I have started to suffer when urinating, I asked Roland in a quiet moment whether he had experienced anything similar. He had, so I decided this morning to air the topic at breakfast. The others, girls as well as boys, admitted to having the same pains and looked relieved that the cause had been identified.

'It's probably the wrong sort of vinegar,' said Howard. 'Let's try balsamic.' He was shouted down. We agreed to return to fruit juice.

After breakfast Dennis drove Joy to the out-patients' for a check-up on her bottom. This would enable him at last to quiz the consultant, Professor Hornyold, on the contradictory advice as to Joy's condition. When Dennis and Joy returned, Dennis looked more cheerful than he had done for ages. The truth, it appears, is somewhere between the two conflicting accounts. Joy is not dead: so much is clear. A fortiori, she did not (contrary to Dr Zayat's speculation) die of a heart attack. She did have a rectal tumour, which

Professor Hornyold removed, but there was a failure of communication between Hornyold and Dr Pee. Hornyold had not intended to say, in his letter to Pee, that the cancer had spread: the point rather was that he had not performed the radical surgery that he would have done on a younger patient to minimise the risk of its spreading: this would have involved pulling out most of Joy's insides and fitting her with a bag. Dennis pressed Hornyold on the question whether he had written misleadingly or Pee had read incompetently, but Hornyold declined to be drawn. Dennis then thought of demanding sight of the letter but, deciding that there was no point, restricted himself instead to asking for a prognosis. He was confronted with more vagueness: given Joy's age and frailty, she was likely to die of something else – such as a heart attack – before the cancer returned. If and when it did, Hornyold would carry out another operation to keep it at bay.

The upshot is that Joy is not in the antechamber to the beyond, but may be hovering outside the door to the antechamber. Although this falls short of a clean bill, it's a lot better than the erroneous news which Pee insisted on imparting to Joy. That damage now had to be undone.

'Do you remember, darling,' Dennis said to Joy, 'when Dr Pee came round and we talked about your health?'

Joy was playing a piano in the air with her left hand, as she often does. 'No,' she replied. 'Was it awful?'

'It was rather. But anyway it turns out that he got it wrong, and you're fine.'

'Goodo,' Joy said with little interest and continued playing.

Chapter 20

•

In comparison with explaining Bernard's absence to the lynx-eyed Sarah, dealing with Julian and Jemima Wormald, when they Dropped In again on their way back from Suffolk, should have been Enid Blyton, but they proved resiliently suspicious. Given that Sarah is still over here hunting for a flat and could well encounter the Wormalds in London, we had to supply them with the story we had supplied to her, that Bernard had gone on an impromptu cruise after his job in Zürich. The problem was to explain why Amelia had previously told them he had gone golfing in Aldeburgh. We agreed that the simplest solution was to say that she had got muddled, what with Bernard being away so much at the moment.

Sure enough, the issue reared its head. 'A cruise?' Julian boomed like the Albert Hall organ with the bourdon out. 'But Amelia, you said he'd gone to Aldeburgh. You were adamant on the point. You said he'd gone golfing with Biffy. I must say I thought it was damn strange: you don't go golfing in mid-winter. The links was closed of course. Can't think why Bernard chooses to play in Aldeburgh even when it's open: bloody useless course.'

'We went round to the Wentworth,' Jemima chipped in in her Listen With Mother voice, 'and they had no record of Bernard or Biffy.'

'Biffy Walker doesn't play golf. He's been in a wheelchair since 1985, when that goat got him. Terrible incident. God knows where they'd put him in the Wentworth. Biffy, that is. Goat's long gone. I'd have had it put down at the time. You of all people, Amelia, ought to remember the wheelchair: when you first saw Biffy in it, you introduced him as Biffy Wheeler, to red faces all round.'

The communards looked reproachfully at Amelia. None of us ever having met Biffy, we had been unable, when she proposed golfing-with-Biffy for the list of alibis, to point out that his disability made the story implausible.

I made a mental note to ask about the goat: I had heard of getting your goat, but it was unusual for the goat to get you. I have since learnt what happened. Biffy owned a goat called Gottlieb, whom he would 'plug in', as he called it: i.e. he would attach Gottlieb by a chain to a metal stake and stick the stake into the lawn. Gottlieb would then nibble all the grass in the circle whose radius was the chain. This done, Biffy would plug him into another part of the lawn and repeat the process until Gottlieb had mowed the whole lawn. In a benign cycle, the emptying of the grassbox (so to speak) provided fertiliser. The only thing wrong with the system was that you got circles instead of stripes. On the fateful day in '85, Biffy failed to plug Gottlieb in firmly enough: Gottlieb, noticing some delicious washing on the line, bolted towards it, thereby uprooting the stake, which flew through the air, biffed Biffy on the back of the neck and paralysed him from there down and then on.

Amelia tittered. 'Oh, I meant Boffy.'

'Boffy?' The Albert Hall organist had his foot hard down on the swell pedal. 'I thought I knew all Bernard's pals, certainly the golfing ones.'

Julian let the matter drop, but later had a word with Dennis and me. 'I say, Bernard isn't in any sort of trouble, is he? This Aldeburgh golfing stuff is decidedly whiffy.' (What with Biffy and Boffy, whiffy was going too far.) 'There was that trouble between the bank and those Italians, the year before he retired.' Dennis and I exchanged pained glances. '*The Sunday Times* tried to make something of it. God, if they'd known a quarter of the truth! Two of Bernie's fellow directors resigned under a cloud, and that Eyetie Pazzi, or whatever his name was, topped himself. I'd hate to think that Bernie was under the River Alde wearing concrete boots. Your firm was tainted, as I remember, Dennis.'

Dennis became pompous. 'The report showed that we'd acted with complete propriety throughout.'

Julian chortled world-wearily. 'Yes of course. No need to get huffy, old chap.'

Biffy, Boffy, whiffy, and now huffy: where would it end? To avoid being driven mad by this thought, I said, 'Surely the thing has blown over after all these years?' I knew the answer to that question.

'That volcano will erupt again sooner or later. If the proverbial hits the fan,' (proverbial what? lava?) 'a lot of people, including Bernard, will find themselves sharing a bed with a horse's head. Better than sharing it with an old cow, as many of them do. Ha ha ha ha.'

Jemima was concerned less about Bernard than about Amelia. 'She's always been a bit vague, I know, but you'd think she'd know where her own husband was. It's hard to confuse Aldeburgh with Zürich, or a round or two of golf with a world cruise. I'd encourage her to see the doctor:

there's a lot they can do these days to slow down senile dementia.' She pronounced it 'demenssia'. 'Aluminium saucepans don't help.'

I hoped Bunny had not heard the last bit; otherwise all the saucepans would be in the dustbin, and Segunda out of the door, before any of us could say Jack Robinson.

Jemima took the opportunity to segue into some bigotry. 'You don't want to end up relying on Care in the Community. It's a joke, really, isn't it?' She smiled sweetly. 'I've heard they use "in the Community" nowadays as a synonym for crazy. Those down-and-outs shouting profanities and pulling their trousers down in the street. They should be locked up out of harm's way.'

As the Wormalds got into the car to leave, Julian murmured to me, 'Remember, if Bernie's up to something, keep your distance.'

'Bye now,' chirruped Jemima. The tyres of their oversized BMW made the gravel roar.

What is the point of adding 'now' to 'bye'? Sue MacGregor used to do it at the end of *Woman's Hour*. Equally irritatingly, she used to start the programme with 'And'. I suppose 'Bye now' is less ghastly than 'Cheers now', the phrase my head of department used, with straw bonhomie, to end his phone calls. A vulgarian as well as an academic charlatan.

Chapter 21

•

Barbara is keener than Amelia to pursue a theme in her education: when the dabbling Amelia sprang from opera to psychology and therapy, Barbara doggedly progressed from dance and movement to tap-dancing. This has the advantage that her deformed but normally bare feet are occasionally encased in tap-shoes, but on balance it's even worse than D&M, for Barbara maliciously continues to practise in her room: it sounds as if a woodman is slowly emptying a large trailer of logs on to the bare floorboards. Concentration on my work having this morning become a lost cause for that reason, I decided to take a turn on the exercise cycle in the gym, choosing Barbara of course for the victim of the imaginary electric current that I would generate with the flywheel.

I was startled to find Roland there, partly because his decrepitude militates against exercise, partly because he is vociferously contemptuous of the modern craze for fitness. He appeared to have been crucified, but it turned out that he had become trapped on the machine for building your pecs, his hands having been caught by the levers which had swung back too far. His dishabille shockingly revealed the ravages of osteoporosis: his spine, the nodules of which were stuck with sweat to his singlet, formed a horseshoe.

'If you had told me you were going to have a work-out,' I said as I prised him free, 'I'd have warned you against the pecs machine. Howard has just been "repairing" it.'

Amelia's smile remained in place. 'Poor Joy,' she said, 'it's very sad,' and applied herself to the gravy.

Chapter 22

•

Last weekend Sarah was back again. After Saturday lunch she set off for one of her walks – she moves in racing style, arms swinging like the wings of a flustered chicken – while the rest of us, with the exception of Joy and Dennis, dispersed for our naps. Joy had wandered off somewhere and the worried Dennis, having looked in vain for her all over the house (he started with my room, which unaccountably is still her favourite), went out to continue his hunt in the garden. By the time we reconvened at teatime in the drawing-room, Dennis was very anxious, for he had also been unable to find her outside. Joy's spontaneous and solitary excursions are as disruptive as those of Jeeves, who occasionally manages to elude Bunny's suffocating clutches: last time he made it, despite his derisory legs (he appears to move on wheels), to the next village, where he was apprehended ripping through a sack of rubbish with his teeth.

We were girding ourselves to form a search party for Joy when Sarah came in from her walk, leading Joy by the hand.

'Thank God!' cried Dennis. 'Joy, my love, where have you been?'

Joy looked at him severely and said, 'Where's Dennis?' Her knees were grubby and the tight on one of them was torn.

'I found her kneeling on top of that big new mound in the pets' cemetery,' said Sarah. 'She was calling "Bernard, Bernard" into the ground.' Sarah gazed round at us before fixing her eyes on Amelia. 'What, or who, is under that mound, Mother?'

Amelia smiled up vacantly from her chair by the fire. 'I'm sorry, dear, I didn't hear you.'

'Yes you did. I asked you what, or who, is under the mound.' She continued to stare, most laser-like, into her mother's eyes. The effect was to paralyse Amelia, who likewise continued to smile vacantly up at her. After a pause Sarah continued, her voice soft and controlled as usual, 'Last time I was here I said as a joke that I thought you had murdered Dad and hidden the corpse. Now I'm not so sure it *is a* joke.' She looked round at the rest of us, before fixing her stare on Amelia again. 'There's something odd going on here. Let's review the facts: whenever I'm here, Dad is absent and you come up with some flimsy reason why. When I came over with Angus in the autumn, you started by saying you didn't know where Dad was; then you told me he was in Liechtenstein, but you didn't have any contact details. When I arrived this time, you said Dad was in London. Then you changed your story: he was in Zürich for a board meeting. Again you didn't have contact details. This board meeting, unlike any other I have heard of, went on for a week. When I managed to extract Dad's mobile number from you, I spoke to someone who, now I think of it, didn't sound a bit like Dad.'

I threw an I-told-you-so look at the others who had put me up to it.

Sarah pressed on. 'He said he had laryngitis. But there was more wrong with the voice than that: it just wasn't Dad's way of talking. I don't think it was Dad at all: it was some

lunatic or criminal pretending to be Dad.' (Lunatic or criminal, yet.) 'Meanwhile the longest board meeting in history
has transformed itself into a world cruise, which Dad is currently supposed to be enjoying in the company of some old
friend I have never heard of with a stupid name – Stuffy or
something.'

Roland, alone among the rest of us, was not too terrified
to speak, but his intervention was unhelpful. 'A lot of your
father's friends have stupid names: there's Cackles, Biffy...'

'And that's another thing: Biffy. I met Jemima Wormald
in town, who said she thought you were going senile because you gave her and Julian such a confused account of
Dad's whereabouts. You told them that he and Biffy had
gone to Aldeburgh for some golf. The Wormalds go to Aldeburgh and find no trace of either of them. And how is Biffy
supposed to play golf? With a club between his teeth?'

Sarah paused, but continued to stare at her mother; then
she bent down so that their faces were only 18 inches apart.
With their jutting chins, they looked like a pair of Deltic
locomotives parked end to end in a siding. 'What I want to
know is this: what the hell is going on? Where is Dad?'

Amelia appeared to be hypnotised. She was unable to
speak or to avert her eyes from Sarah's. Her smile had modulated from vacant to queasy, her complexion (so far as visible under her rouge) had gone yellow, and her head had
started to wobble. There was a good ten seconds' electric
silence. Then Sarah said, even more softly than before, in a
voice at once coaxing and menacing: 'Is he under that
mound?'

It was a bravura performance: if Sarah had not been a

journalist, she would have been an ace in MI5. A tear rolled out of one of Amelia's eyes and left a furrow in the impasto of her rouge. Blood out of a stone is as nothing to a tear out of Amelia.

Sarah straightened up and briskly addressed us all. 'I'm going to ask Mr Shanks to dig the mound up.'

Some of us exchanged panic-stricken glances. Others gawped helplessly at Sarah, as Amelia was still doing. Dennis was standing 'at ease', staring out of the window into the gathering dusk. Joy, unsupervised, was gobbling the biscuits. Her tendency to hoover up food when given the chance is another trait she shares with Jeeves.

It seemed that no-one was going to do anything to try and save the situation, so I pulled myself together enough to say, 'This is ridiculous, Sarah. I don't think any of us knows what's under the mound.' I decided that lying couldn't make things any worse. 'It's probably something Mr Shanks has done that relates to the garden – compost or what have you.'

I was aware that, when we had inhumed Bernard, we had toyed with putting it about that Amelia had agreed to let a friend bury a big dog, but it seemed to me that to say this would merely trigger another battery of questions from Sarah. Which friend? What dog?

She dismissed my interjection. 'Mr Shanks has worked here for years. He wouldn't turn the pets' cemetery into a compost heap. Anyway, there's a perfectly good heap by the herb garden.'

Howard butted in. 'Your mother kindly agreed to let a friend bury a big dog there.' I glared at him.

'What? Which friend?' Sarah turned back to Amelia. 'What dog?'

Amelia returned the queasy smile which had never left her lips even after the tear had intaglioed her make-up.

'Kierkegaard,' said Roland heartily. 'A Great Dane.' He had made this joke before and was clearly pleased with it, but none of the rest of us thought that now was the moment.

'I'm not listening to any more of this,' said Sarah. 'As I say, I'm going to get Mr Shanks to dig up the mound.'

'You can't!' I cried automatically.

'Why not?'

I heard myself say: 'He's in bed with sciatica.'

'Rubbish. I saw him spiking the lawn today.'

'That's what did his back in,' said Roland.

'It was half an hour ago.'

Dennis turned round from the window. 'Sarah, my dear, it's nearly dark. You can't ask Mr Shanks to do anything now. Let's sleep on it and decide in the morning.'

Given Dennis's refusal so far to have anything to do with the plot, this intervention was as generous as it was judicious. I felt like kissing him. The urge went away as I remembered the time he leered at me from behind a shrub.

'Sleep on the mound?' said Sarah (sometimes Homer nods). 'Oh – I see. All right then, in the morning. But I'm not letting this drop. If Mr Shanks is out of action, I'll find someone else to do the digging.' She turned to Amelia and said severely, 'I'll be in my room, Mum. I've got to phone Angus about apartments.' Then she stalked out of the room.

There was a dazed silence for half a minute thereafter; then I went to the door and closed it.

'So now what?' said Roland.

Bunny started to whimper. 'Oh dear, we're all going to prison. I can't bear it.'

'Pull yourself together, for Christ's sake.'

Bunny's admirer was more sympathetic than her husband: Howard tried to put his arm round her, but she shook it off and scowled at him. At least this latest unwelcome advance stopped her whimpering.

Amelia, after her grilling, had recovered her poise and some of her natural colour. 'We'll have to move Bernard during the night,' she declared.

'What do you mean?' said Howard, keen to distract the general attention from his rebuff.

'What do you think I mean?' Amelia used her sweetest cocktail-party voice.

Barbara: 'Dig him up? Heaven help us!'

Amelia beamed graciously. One has to admire the woman's sangfroid. There was a silence while we savoured the proposal's full gruesomeness. The savour moved me to say, 'You can count me out, so far as digging is concerned. After burying Bernard, I couldn't bend for a fortnight.'

'Weigh up the options, old man,' said Roland. 'You won't have *room* to bend in a prison cell – especially if you're sharing it with Howard. I, on the other hand, will have no option but to bend, the way my spine's gone. The upside is that they'll give me a cell of my own.'

'I'm not doing any more digging either,' Howard said. 'And I can't see any prospect of you volunteering, Roland.' He was nettled by the jibe about his girth – a running gag from Roland and others.

'In that case,' said Barbara, 'we'll need outside help.'

'Oh yes – easy to find.'

'Oik.'

This inspired monosyllable was emitted by Joy, who combined it with a belch – the result of eating all those biscuits. We turned to her in admiration, but she was now abstractedly playing her piano in the air with her left hand.

'Oik spends his days digging roads,' said Roland. 'He'll have Bernard up in a trice. And he's just the evil bastard for this sort of job. We'll have to pay him to shut up, of course. A hundred quid should do it. You're his buddy, Dennis: you'll have to do the talking.'

'I have told you from the start that I'm having nothing to do with this illegal, immoral and sordid scheme.'

'You just involved yourself in it by helping us buy time from Sarah,' I replied. I had some score-settling to do with Dennis in the matter of consistency between principle and conduct.

'Try explaining that to the police,' added Barbara.

'We're all *so* grateful to you, Dennis,' said Amelia, as if she were now thanking the host of the cocktail party.

The result of the discussion was that at one a.m. I was standing by Bernard's grave with Howard, Oik, some digging implements and a torch. Roland was sitting up in the drawing-room to deal with Sarah if by any chance she should come downstairs; in the unlikely event that Sarah, despite Roland's efforts to distract her, should decide on some outdoor exercise in the small hours, Amelia and Barbara were posted respectively near the front and the back door to hurry over to the grave and warn us; and Bunny was posted on the lawn to watch Sarah's window and raise the alarm if her light came on. Dennis and Joy had gone to bed after Dennis, with vociferous misgivings, had knocked up Oik and enlisted him for the £100. There had been some debate as to whether this was the right amount: if we offered too little, Oik would not be moved to help; if too much, he would realise how frightened we were and perhaps try to exploit the situation. I was surprised that Dennis had allowed himself to be persuaded: perhaps his softer feelings, at the thought of his friends being led away in irons, had prevailed over his principles; or perhaps he feared that, if the plot were discovered, he would find it hard to convince the authorities that he had not been involved. Barbara's 'Try explaining that to the police' had probably been a threat to shop him: relations between the two have never recovered since she accused him of playing the pink oboe.

I would have been happier (to be more accurate: less wretchedly anxious) if Dennis had stuck around to keep Oik under control, for I feared that Oik would either cleave my skull in twain with a spade or, at the very least, whip out his lighter again and finish incinerating my chin. My unease was heightened by the fact that, despite the freezing cold, Oik had nothing on except his underpants, a pair of ex-army boots and the luminescent orange waistcoat he wears when working on the roads. This last he must have put on automatically, for its inappropriateness to the present job should have been obvious even to one with his single-digit IQ. The pong of his aftershave drowned the pleasant odours of the night. Oik was taciturn as usual but clearly tickled by the fact that the seemingly respectable elderly residents of The Graylings were complicit in a crime so heinous, his stunted feeling for irony issuing in the odd remark during the digging, such as 'Fucking bunch of crook perverts, you old fuckers. Fucking respectable, aren't ya.' He spat, and added 'Cunts.' Howard and I declined to reply, partly because we didn't want to provoke him, partly because the digging didn't leave us enough breath. I had been firm with Howard this time and made sure that he actually dug: there was to be no repeat of the burial, when his contribution had been cosmetic.

We were about two feet down, and bracing ourselves for an encounter with whatever was left of Bernard, when there was a rustle in the bushes and some grunting, as if a wild boar were about to charge. Oik muttered 'Fucking cunt' and adopted combat position with a pickaxe, while I shone the torch at the source of the noise. Bunny emerged, then shrieked and ducked as Oik lunged at her with the axe. Howard and I went Shshshsh by reflex, and Oik muttered 'Fucking cunt' again as he lowered his weapon in disappointment.

'Bunny, thank God it's you,' gasped Howard. 'We heard your pants.' I was too tense and tired to relish the ambiguity of this sentence.

'Her light's on,' Bunny agitatedly whispered between her pants. 'What if she comes down? You'd better hide. Oh Lord!'

I reminded her of the other layers of defence in the form of Roland, Amelia and Barbara, but suggested that we go on to the lawn in any case and have a look. There was a light on upstairs but, as I pointed out to Bunny with some acerbity, it was in the window of Dennis's and Joy's room, not Sarah's. We were detained from returning immediately to work by the silhouettes cast, in the manner of Nang Yai, on the curtains: Joy's shadow was doing some ballet, Dennis's some semaphore. Perhaps Dennis was trying to communicate something to us; more likely he was putting on this grotesque display to gratify some whim of Joy's. It's a wonder he has not had a nervous breakdown if he has to do this sort of thing night after night.

Before leaving Bunny to resume her watch on the lawn, I pointed out Sarah's window to her, then checked Bunny's understanding by asking her to point it out to me. On the third attempt she got it right and Howard, Oik and I went back to our digging. After another quarter of an hour's work, my spade met something spongy. Shuddering, I scraped away the soil in the vicinity and switched on the torch, which revealed a patch of tweed. Despite the foreseeable results of Sarah's discovering our plot, I was strongly tempted to shovel back the soil and bog off: I doubted I could face the sight of Bernard's rotting corpse, let alone the prospect of manhandling it. Some more digging and scraping brought Bernard into full view: I took care not to shine the torch at his face, but could see enough to realise that decomposition had gone a fair way. I was on the verge of retching. Howard went well over the verge (as he had over the grass one with the Gadabout) and was generously sick on the corpse, prompting further donnish wit from Oik.

It had been agreed that we would not try to bury the body somewhere else: we didn't have enough time or energy and a reinterment would create a new mound which Sarah might discover in turn. The plan was to hide Bernard temporarily under the compost heap and fill in the grave: the next morning Sarah would get Mr Shanks to dig the grave up; they would find nothing; Mr S would fill the grave in; when they were both out of the way, we would dig it up, reinsert Bernard and fill it in again; then, with luck, Bernard could rest in peace.

Heaving Bernard out of the grave and dragging him to the compost heap was a test of fortitude, physical and psychological: this time we had been unable to find any plastic sheeting in Mr Shanks's shed, so we had to lay hands on the corpse – an ordeal even for the insensate Oik. We tried to restrict ourselves to pulling Bernard by the edge of his clothes, but could not get a purchase, so Oik and Howard grabbed him by the shoulders while I took hold of his ankles. Again I nearly retched as I felt how bony they had become. A foul smell, which even Oik's aftershave couldn't mask, erupted as we started to move the corpse: this time I did retch, as did Oik, and Howard vomited another bucketful. It is astonishing – come to think of it, it isn't – how much his stomach holds.

We completed the operation at five a.m. To avoid waking Sarah, I eschewed the hot and muscle-relaxing bath I yearned for and lay down in my filth on the bed, plunging instantly into a deep sleep. I dreamt that the grave had expanded to the width of a double bed and that Bernard and I were lying in it side by side. He turned to me and leered, as Dennis had done from behind the shrub: Bernard's face had rotted away to the bone, and worms were crawling out of his nostrils, ears and mouth. Sarah was glaring down at us from the grave-side: 'So,' she said, 'you two are mattress-munchers. Dennis told me.' – 'I'm not having anything to do with these illegal, immoral and sordid goings-on,' the voice of Dennis said from somewhere. Bernard sat up in the grave: 'It's not illegal any more,' he said in a distant and echoing voice, 'but I can't get blood into my Johnson. It's drained away.' He spat worms out as he was talking. Amelia appeared at the grave-side: the furrow in her rouge, left by the tear, had changed direction and multiplied, so that her cheeks were like those of an African tribeswoman. 'You two darlings need to be covered up,' she said in the cocktail-party voice, and threw a large shovelful of soil down on Bernard and me. As it hit my face, I sat up with a cry and woke up. I really had sat up with a cry.

I had been asleep for three hours and, as my gingerly attempts to move revealed quickly and painfully, was now even stiffer than I had been after Bernard's burial: you could have used me for one of those stunts of hypnotism in which the stooge stays rigid when propped across two trestles. To get down to breakfast I resorted to the Escalope but, as a result of one of Howard's attempts to improve its performance, it was buggered and conked out on the first floor, so I had to stagger the rest of the way down, holding on to the banister with both hands and, like an infant, putting both feet on each step before moving down to the next one. Howard himself made it downstairs on his bottom.

The conversation at breakfast was sparse and muted, as Sarah was present and we were all anxiously waiting for her to, and still praying that she would not, announce that she was off to solicit Mr Shanks's help in digging up the mound. It only now occurred to me that Mr S was likely to take a Dim View of being asked to do this on a Sunday, or even at all: if he refused, and Sarah could enlist no-one else that day, she would doubtless stay on at The Graylings until she did find someone to do the job: in that case Bernard would meanwhile be lying, easily discoverable, under a thin layer of compost – for the heap had turned out to be sadly depleted. It had already occurred to me that there was a danger of Sarah's noticing that the mound had been freshly tampered with: the grass that had started to grow over it was obliterated by our activities, and there might be footprints and drag marks from the mound to the heap. We, or at least I, had been careful to cover our traces, but there's a limit to what you can do when you are shaken and exhausted and only have a torch to see by. I had just decided to slink down to the grave straight after breakfast, to tidy up before Sarah and Mr Shanks had time to get there, when Sarah announced, 'I've spoken to Mr Shanks. He's at the mound already, making a start. He said he was glad to help, as he thought the mound was suspicious. I'm going down now to see how he's getting on.'

So it was a matter of wachet, betet, seid bereit. Amelia and Howard went into the drawing-room with the papers, Bunny took Jeeves into the garden so that he could relieve himself (the dispute over the turds around the house is still raging, so Bunny is vigilant in protecting her position), and the rest of us dispersed to our rooms. I was too tired to work, so I settled down with a book on the criminal prosecution and capital punishment of animals, which a judge had lent to me (he reads it on the lavatory). I soon felt myself nodding off, but tried to resist, as I was frightened of drifting back into that dreadful dream of being in the grave with Bernard.

I was restored to full wakefulness by the slamming of the front door followed by a shriek from the hall of 'Mother! Mother!' It could only be Sarah, but I didn't recognise the voice, for till then I had never heard her speak above piano, let alone shriek. My heart started to pound (if this level of excitement went on much longer, I would have an attack more massive than Bernard's) and, like an insect drawn to the flame, I went on to the landing to look down to the hall. At the same moment Barbara burst from her room, like a breeze block fired from a catapult, barged past me and thundered downstairs. On the landing below, Roland, Bunny and Dennis were already peering down; Joy peered up at me and gave a dignified wave, like the Queen.

We had an aerial view of Sarah looking around distraughtly in the middle of the hall and then of Jeeves shooting out from the kitchen (he must have come in through the back door), across the hall and into the coat cupboard, whence he howled uncannily. Jeeves was pursued into the cupboard, at a slower pace, by Bunny, whose wheezing I could hear even from my eyrie. Sarah turned towards the drawing-room door, cried, 'There you are!' and strode in, followed by Barbara, who had now reached the ground floor. Further shrieks were heard from the drawing-room; then Sarah came back into our line of sight, dragging Amelia by the wrist, while Amelia twittered and struggled to get back into the drawing-room: it was as if Sarah were

the mother and Amelia her rebellious toddler. 'You're damn
well coming to see!' shouted Sarah. 'You're coming now!'
While this tug-of-war was going on, Bunny came back into
view on the opposite side of the hall, dragging Jeeves out
of the coat cupboard. The symmetry was satisfying.

Sarah now had the front door open again and was pulling
Amelia through it. Barbara was close on their tail, shouting,
'Stop it, you beast! You're hurting her!' Howard came hob-
bling after. Bunny joined them, Jeeves shot back into the
cupboard and the rest of us started trundling downstairs,
like schoolchildren between classes. We would have done
better to run back into our rooms and hide, but the residents of The Graylings are sheep, or rather Great Auks, who
followed each other along the plank to execution and ex-
tinction.

We formed a straggling procession as we crossed the lawn
to the compost heap. On the way we passed the grave: it
was half dug-up, the implements were scattered in a way
that indicated they had been abandoned in a hurry, and
there was no sign of Mr Shanks. As I had feared, there were
drag marks from the grave to the heap. Sticking out of the
heap was the head of Bernard, the face pointed sideways,
so that he was looking straight at us as we approached, like
the magician's assistant who smiles out of a box at the audience while the magician saws her in half. Bernard, however, was not smiling: he wore the look of outraged
astonishment – eyes and mouth wide open – that he had
worn when we buried him; but now his face was black,
partly from earth, partly from decomposition. His cheeks
had sunk and his mouth was horribly large, as the lips had

started to erode, but at least there were no worms crawling from his orifices. For a moment we all stared at this apparition, with the exception of Bunny who stood at the back, looking away and whining, 'I've already seen it: I can't bear to look again.'

Sarah, who still had Amelia in her grasp, stood closer to the projecting head than any of us cared to do. 'We owe this discovery to Bunny's dog,' she said in a voice that had resumed its customary softness, although a quaver was audible. 'Mr Shanks and I were by the mound – grave, I should now say – when we heard yapping.' Bunny's eyebrows furrowed at Sarah's choice of verb. 'We walked over to see what was going on and found the dog scrabbling at the compost heap.'

'He's got a name,' Bunny murmured to herself. 'He's called Jeeves.'

'When we looked more closely, we found that it had uncovered part of a face.' Bunny's eyebrows furrowed more deeply, at Sarah's choice of pronoun. 'Mr Shanks fetched his spade and cleared away some more compost, with the result you can all see. As you can imagine, he is very upset and has gone back to his cottage.' Sarah paused. 'Mother, you're coming with me back to the house, where we are going to have a long talk. I'd be grateful if two of the men would cover the face again till the police get here.'

We looked at each other in dismay at the mention of the police.

'Have you called the police yet, Sarah?' Dennis asked in a manner admirably measured.

'Not yet, no. Why?'

'I think you should wait, before doing so, until you have had the talk with your mother.'

Sarah treated Dennis to one of her laser beam stares. 'I'll bear in mind what you say,' she replied coldly and then started hauling Amelia, whose wrist was still in her grip, back to the house.

Dennis and Roland then turned to Howard and me with looks that said, 'It's an accepted fact that you two are the manual labourers in this community, so get cracking with the spades.' But Howard refused to lift a finger and hobbled away across the lawn, leaving me to push compost under and over poor Bernard's rotting head until it was hidden from view.

Lunch was an even more subdued affair than breakfast had been. Sarah and Amelia were shut away in Amelia's bedroom (at various points in the previous hour, assorted communards had happened to find themselves outside the bedroom door, but mother and daughter were speaking too quietly for us to learn anything) and none of the rest of us had any appetite for conversation: with the likely exception of Joy, each of us was perpending the consequences of Sarah's turning the matter over to the police. I cursed myself for ever having suggested the idea of a commune: if I had kept my big mouth shut, I could now be sitting comfortably, securely and in contented solitude by a bar-fire in a bedsit, eating baked beans on toast while reading about the prosecution and capital punishment of animals. Instead, I faced the prospect of spending my final years in the slammer, sharing a cell with some Oik-like figure – possibly Oik himself. The image conjured up by Roland, of my being squeezed into a cell with Howard, and with no room to bend, was enticing in comparison. Our appetite for food had likewise dwindled: only Howard could bring himself to eat seconds, and even he helped himself to less than usual; but he compensated by increasing his dose of booze, downing a bottle and a half of wine by himself, which caused his face to become shiny and his eyes piggish. We then dispersed again to our rooms, like Trappists leaving the refectory.

At teatime the gong sounded repeatedly and urgently, as it had when Bunny tolled it for Bernard's death. This time the toller was Sarah, who was wasting her energy as we were all coming down to tea anyway. Amelia, who was already installed in her seat by the drawing-room fire, had assumed her majesty again and beamed beatifically at us as she reached over to the trolley to pour the tea. I noticed an angry red ring around her wrist. The pouring done and the biscuits distributed, she settled back, closed her eyes and smiled serenely, as if listening to a sublime piece of music. In fact what we had to listen to was another speech from Sarah, who was standing next to her mother with her elbow on the mantelpiece, in the posture adopted by the Cambridge Apostles when they are giving talks. When I was an undergraduate at Trinity Hall I used to practise this position in the hope of being invited to become an Apostle, but the call never came.

'After a lot of difficulty,' Sarah announced, 'I think I've got to the bottom of this. You all plotted to hide Dad's death because you thought that when I inherited The Graylings I would kick you out.'

'Not "all",' interrupted Dennis, but she ignored him.

'It says a lot about what you think of me. Mum must have painted a pretty picture.' (Amelia's eyes remained closed and her smile serene.) 'After the vile thing you have done, that's exactly what you deserve – not just to be dismissed from this place but to be handed over to the police.' She paused to savour our squirming. 'If I don't report you, I'll be a party to the crime. So I'm afraid I have no option.'

The sanctimonious bitch was disguising her vindictiveness as rectitude. Roland muttered something under his breath, presumably along those lines. Bunny and Howard started to cry. Dennis hid his face in his hands. Barbara stared bitterly at her bunions. Only Joy and Amelia kept their composure: Joy was again playing the piano in the air with her left hand (did she ever study the Ravel concerto and, if so, did it have some special meaning for her?) and was running her tongue slowly over her teeth. Amelia continued her impersonation of Buddha: her calm, in face of the impending disaster, was magnificent or idiotic.

'To be more exact,' Sarah went on, 'I have no *legal* option other than to report this to the police.' She paused again. 'But I must weigh legal obligation against family feeling. As you can imagine, I'm not overjoyed at the thought of handing over my mother and her closest friends, even when they have behaved so abominably. So, if I can be sure that you will keep quiet, we can keep the police out of it. I think my contacts are good enough to ensure that the formalities of Dad's death are completed without exciting suspicion.' The crying of Bunny and Howard became more extravagant. 'You can leave the rest to me. No-one should go near the compost heap again till I say so.'

when they returned from Cambridge, but Roland came into the drawing-room alone and brooding, and his face had even more of the death-mask than could be attributed to Parkinson's. When Bunny crisply asked him whether he had enjoyed himself, he didn't reply but went over to the drinks cabinet, poured himself a gargantuan Scotch and then, without having said a word to any of us, went off to bed.

The next morning he was no less surly at breakfast, after which I saw him and Howard stalking off together down the drive. There seemed to be Peggy trouble, but I could not work out why the subject should bring Roland and Howard together, as their interests conflicted. They returned in time for lunch, at which it was noticeable that they both smelt of beer and that neither spoke to or even looked at the other. Howard was overjolly with everyone else, but Roland's mood had darkened to deep black. The rest of us carried on as if nothing were wrong, for it's now the norm at The Graylings that at any one time at least two of the residents are squabbling.

After lunch I went upstairs to write. The laptop had just made itself ready when I heard the whirr of the Escalope: it increased in volume and pitch, there was a clank, then a grunt, then a half-second's silence, then a muttered 'Shit' accompanied by the sound of staggering. Today, I decided, I was not going to permit Howard to erode my valuable time with his self-obsessed maundering: I would put my foot down and politely but firmly ask him to leave.

There was a knock, which I ignored. The door opened anyway and Roland walked in. I gave him a look of unwelcoming inquiry.

'I'm sorry to interrupt – I know how irritating it is. But I need to talk to you.'

I gestured at the empty chair. He sat down and came straight to the point. 'Did you know about Bunny and Howard?'

I didn't have time to reflect on the pros and cons of telling the truth, so I deflected the question with another. 'What do you mean?'

'That they have been having an affair for years.'

I tried to keep an impassive look on my face and to answer steadily. 'No, I didn't know that. What makes you think it's true?'

'To be more precise: three affairs and an abortion.'

'Who told you that?'

He started brooding and didn't answer for a while. 'What? Peggy said something, so I pressed Howard for details and he blurted it all out.'

I was amazed that even Howard could have been so stupid as to confide this secret to Peggy and that Peggy could have been so tactless as to have passed it on to Roland. Perhaps she was playing a larger game.

'Apparently they started when Kath left him. We'd only been married a couple of years. He said the other affairs took place too when he was between wives, but I shouldn't think it was as clean as that. He had all those other women.'

I could not think of anything to say. Misery seemed to have accelerated the process of shrinking and bending Roland that osteoporosis had already got well under way. He looked like a foetus, and just as vulnerable.

'How could I have missed it all these years?' he went on.

'Half a century of betrayal. It's the effect it has on your memories. It undermines them. The whole of our past has been a lie. The whole of our adult life.'

'You've had enough affairs of your own over the years.'

Roland had never made much effort to conceal these from Bunny. One of his bits of fluff he even brought into their home as a 'secretary': to add further insult to the insult that he had already added to injury, the girl was a near-perfect replica of the Bunny of 20 years earlier. 'He has traded me in for a new model,' Bunny ruefully commented at the time.

Roland glared at me: he had come for sympathy. 'It's different. She knew about those.'

'That makes it better?'

'We had an understanding.'

'You mean she put up with it.' There was another pause. 'It's Bunny I feel sorry for: you've both exploited her.'

'And now it turns out she's been exploiting me. For what it's worth, she betrayed me first.'

'That's playground talk.'

'We can't all go on living here. I can't sit at the same table as that bastard, pretending nothing's happened. I don't think I want to go on living with Bunny. Perhaps I'll find a flat.'

'You need her. You need each other. You're both old.'

'When I need a nurse, I'll get a nurse,' Roland snapped.

I would have liked to say that it was all a long time ago, that we were all past that sort of thing and that we could move on. But the facts wouldn't bear it: only recently I had witnessed Howard breathing heavily over Bunny, and he and Roland were sparring over Peggy like a couple of stags in season. They are both still strapped to a lunatic. So I lamely said, 'Don't do anything hasty. The commune's quite a precious thing, for all its horrors.'

'It's a madhouse.'

'Better folie à huit than solitary desolation.'

'Passionate and impulsive: that's what Amelia's personality test said about Howard. I might have known.'

'Women's-magazine parlour game: that's what you said about the personality test.'

'I ought to thump him.'

'Your fist would sink into a roll of flesh.'

A wan smile crossed Roland's face as he got up. 'Don't say anything.' He was very shaky. As he walked to the door, he tripped on the hem of his trousers, which were now too long for him.

'With a couple of loudhailers like Howard and Peggy, I shan't need to.' But Roland looked imploring, so I added, 'Of course not.'

Chapter 24

•

Our gratitude to Sarah, for her magnanimous reaction to
the concealment of Bernard, soon faded into complacency,
and by the time she returned to New York the whole ghastly
sequence of events – the burial, the increasingly desperate
alibis, the impersonation down the phone, the exhumation
of the decaying corpse – seemed a silly nightmare that was
fading in the memory. As Bernard's death is now official,
Amelia's withers were unwrung when she opened the following letter addressed to Bernard:

Egregio Signore,

You are living since a long time. We think you are
wanting to live longer time. So we respectably aks
you pay your Italian debts. We are knowing you are
knowing watt we mean and how much. We kindly
aks you phone please this number to arrange deliv-
erance.

There followed a mobile phone number. The letter was un-
signed, there was no letterhead and the envelope bore a
Naples postmark.

'I phoned the number,' Amelia told me blithely. 'I was
very polite. So was the chap at the other end: he seemed
awfully nice, though his accent was rather thick. I said I was
sorry, but Bernard had died, and so I couldn't help. I also

said I was sure Bernard couldn't owe him any money: Bernie was always prompt with his payments – he had direct debit, you know. I wished the nice Italian the best of luck in collecting his other debts.' She tinkled with laughter and then added, 'I hope he doesn't pester Sarah, after she has been so understanding.' She was still smiling.

And so, with luck, we have shaken off one attempt at extortion. Unfortunately we now face another – less frightening but more pressing, so the expected disutilities, as economists like to say, are much the same. There seems no end to our reaping what we sowed.

'I'm afraid,' Dennis announced at lunch, 'I have some rather bad news. Oik is asking for more money to keep quiet about what we did to Bernard.' It had struck me before as disloyal of Dennis, who is Oik's friend, to go along with our use of this insulting nickname.

Barbara banged down her cutlery. 'Little shit! Christ, I knew it was a mistake to get him involved.'

'You didn't object at the time,' said Howard. 'You joined the chorus praising Joy for her stroke of genius.'

'I didn't. There wasn't a chorus of praise, and it wasn't a stroke of genius. Joy says the first thing that comes into her head – when there's anything in it at all.'

Joy, to the delight of the rest of us, threw a buttery potato at Barbara and hit her on her flat bosom. She was reaching into the vegetable dish to throw a bit of cauliflower, but Dennis caught her in time. While the infuriated Barbara wiped herself down with a napkin she had dipped in the water jug, I said, 'Let's stick to the matter in hand. What is Oik asking for?'

Dennis was about to answer when Segunda came in from the kitchen with some extra gravy. We fell silent and glared at her suspiciously: was she complicit in the scheme of blackmail? The blank look with which she returned our glares suggested not, but who could tell? Oik might have intimidated her into aiding and abetting. When she had gone out, Dennis resumed in a softer voice: 'He says that if the police find out what we did we'll go behind bars, and that it's worth more than a one-off payment of £100 to prevent that. Actually he put it in rather more forceful and less elegant terms, but that was the gist. He says we have plenty of money between us. He wants £500 a week.'

The general outcry was cut short as Segunda came in again: it was as if the Pause button had been pressed during the Anvil Chorus. As soon as she had returned to the kitchen, and before the execrations could continue, Dennis started defending Oik: 'He's not a bad boy. He had the most dreadful childhood.'

This caused another outburst, even louder and more indignant. 'Not a bad boy!' Amelia expostulated. 'He's a hardened criminal. He has been in prison for assault. He was caught with drugs. Heaven knows what undetected crimes he has on his conscience.'

Barbara: 'He hasn't got a conscience.'

Bunny said, 'You're his chum, Dennis. Can't you talk him round?'

'I've tried. It's not easy to make him see reason.'

Roland: 'His behaviour in this matter seems quite reasonable to me.'

Barbara, the former businesswoman, said, 'You can at

least try to bargain with him – get the price down a bit. Say £200.'

Dennis agreed to have a go but was not hopeful. He emphasised the urgency of the situation: Oik was proposing to shop us by the end of the week if we didn't cough up.

'It's bluff,' I said. 'Once he has reported us, he won't get any more cash.'

'Why don't we call *his* bluff?' suggested Roland. 'We just refuse to be intimidated: then he doesn't have anything to gain by going to the police. They'll never believe him in any case.'

'He's not adept in game theory. As Dennis said, and as you seem to deny, Oik can't be relied on to see reason.'

'If we call his bluff over the money,' said Amelia, 'he'll start doing other awful things. He's already stealing from us: he'll get more brazen about it. Or he'll turn violent. Remember Dennis's black eye.' Dennis looked not at all pleased that this incident had been brought up again.

'And the time he went for my face with a lighter,' I added.

Roland: 'Can't we play a trump by threatening to turn him in for something? Amelia's right: he's doubtless guilty of all sorts of crimes the police haven't solved. There was that piece in the local paper this week: some thugs tied up a pensioner in Fyfield and poured HP Sauce over her head before making off with twenty quid. That bears the mark of our friend.'

'That's groundless slander,' said Dennis. 'There's no reason to think that Oik had anything to do with it. He has paid his dues to society.'

Barbara: 'Oh yes – and now he wants to replenish his coffers by relieving us of £500 per week. I can't believe you're defending him when he's attacking you.'

Amelia: 'But even if he has committed other crimes, how can we prove it?'

'We make a bold accusation,' proposed Roland. 'We confront him with the HP Sauce attack and break him down.'

'Pie in the sky,' said Barbara.

'Well, what about Dennis pressing charges for the black eye?'

'Can we please let that matter drop,' barked Dennis.

I speculated on the lurid facts that a trial for the black eye would bring to light. To put Dennis out of his misery, I said, 'Or I could report him for trying to ignite my chin.'

This hardly looked the trump card to which Roland had referred; in any event, as Amelia had already observed, retaliatory action might provoke Oik into other dastardly acts. A vicious spiral could develop. Having run out of ideas, we agreed that Oik would have to be paid until we came up with a better solution. 'It buys us time,' I mused.

'That's just what you said about hiding Bernard,' replied Roland. 'Look where it got us.'

'It turned out all right in the end.'

'Now we're literally buying time.'

'Not me,' said Howard. 'I don't have a penny to spare.'

'Actually, I'm afraid I can't contribute either,' I said.

Dennis, who could see the way the wind was blowing, said, 'It doesn't come to much if we divide it among all of us. Even if I can't get us a reduction, it's only just over £60 a week each.'

'Out of the question,' said Howard.

Barbara rounded on him. 'You could save £60 out of what you allow yourself for drink and fags. If you gave up both, you'd be a billionaire.'

'Let's cut the cackle. We all know Amelia and Dennis are rolling in it. I think they should pay on our behalf.'

Amelia, who eccentrically boasts of being 'frightfully mean', laughed off Howard's proposal. She reminded him that, because of her debts, she had nothing of her own and that, once probate came through, Bernard's estate would go to Sarah: there was still a discussion to be had with Sarah about Amelia's allowance. Dennis said that he had never wanted to touch our plot in the first place and had only intervened to prevent disaster. He was told to change the record. The debate, which was long and increasingly acrimonious, ended with Dennis's grudgingly agreeing to pay Oik, but in the interim only: he would be reimbursed on an equitable basis still to be agreed. 'To be agreed' was optimistic.

Chapter 25

•

Howard's latest wheeze, in his pursuit of well-being, is to go for early-morning swims. There is a heated pool a few miles away, but he doesn't have a car and he claims that the pool anyway isn't spartan enough. (In my view the objection to the pool is its squalor: the floating Elastoplasts and pubic hairs, and the men of our age who furtively hang on to the rail while the water turns yellow around them.) Instead, therefore, he has been taking pre-daybreak dips in the village pond. There must be a bylaw against this, and the pond is anyway ill-suited to swimming, for the water is clogged with weeds, both the water and the grass around are fouled by the ducks and geese, and the pond is too small to enable one to do more than a few strokes. Howard maintains that a few strokes are enough: in winter, he claims, you can only stay alive in the pond, as in the North Sea, for a short while. There may be something in this, for he now has a heavy cold of a style that is typical of the man: despite the massive doses of Segunda's Lem-Sick and the wrapping of his lips round his teeth, Howard's exuberant sneezes shower our plates at meal-times with virus-bearing droplets. I am now feeling rather sniffly.

Yesterday morning, before breakfast, we received a phone call from a Constable Wiggins who requested that someone come down to the village green to collect one Howard who had just been rescued from the pond. Dennis and I drove there and through the gloaming discerned a small group by the water, around them a scattering of ducks and geese who were cackling disgruntledly at having been woken before dawn. In the centre of the group was a policeman – presumably PC Wiggins – and a half-dressed, steaming and snorting Howard. He had got entangled in the weeds, had called out and had been rescued by some public-spirited people who lived on the green. These were now venting their displeasure, one protesting at having been disturbed, another lamenting the adverse effects on the wildlife (the cackling was getting louder), a third asserting that it was a disgrace to go around flashing. This was an overstatement: it turns out that Howard eschews trunks, but there can't have been much on view, given his paunch (or rather, his several rolls), the darkness and the withering effect of the temperature. He was unable to reply effectively, as he had removed for the swim his hearing-aid and his false teeth (his caved-in mouth made him look years older), but the constable managed to calm the complainants down by sternly telling Howard that, if he tried this caper again, he would face charges. I know policemen are always said to look young (from where I'm standing, Law Lords look boyish) but this one was a toddler – an impression reinforced by the fact that his helmet was two sizes too big.

Dennis and I thanked everyone and were ushering Howard to the car when the lady who had accused him of flashing called after us, 'What about his trike?' Howard broke into a doubtfully genuine fit of coughing as she pointed across the pond to a Gadabout. 'Christ Almighty,' Dennis muttered through his teeth, clearly deciding to save an outburst for later. We now faced the problem of getting

the Gadabout home. Howard was in no state to drive anything and, although I have a licence, I was last behind the
wheel of a car in 1962, which made Dennis unwilling to
entrust the Jag to me. The pis aller was for him to give me
a quick lesson on the Gadabout and leave it to me to ride
it back to The Graylings. It was such fun that I'm thinking
of getting one – or perhaps Dennis will lend me his now
and then. Probably best not to ask for a day or two.

When I arrived home, the house was in uproar. The focus
of attention was Bunny, who was sobbing uncontrollably
while Amelia tried to coax her into drinking some sweet
tea. My first thought, in the light of recent revelations, was
that this was an overreaction to the peril that Howard had
been in, but Dennis whispered that Jeeves had been found
dead in the utility-room. There were assorted speculations
on the cause: Jeeves was not old, but perhaps the crushing
of his ribs by Howard had done some undetected internal
damage, or the scratching of his eye by Moth had caused
blood-poisoning, or perhaps his nerves had given way.
Those of us who still had working memories, and had witnessed the last battle between the pets, remembered Barbara's threat to kill Jeeves, but we had shrugged it off as a
discharge of anger. Now we were less sure, and our suspi-
cions were reinforced by Barbara's conspicuous absence:
usually in an emergency she is the first to wade in. Dennis
reminded me that Barbara had recently been making a song
and dance about a mouse and had put out some trays of
poison in the larder: it would have been easy enough for
her, while she was at it, to sprinkle some on to Jeeves's
Chum.

We were unable to pursue this speculation, for after breakfast Dennis had to go out in the car again, this time to drop Joy off at the day centre which takes her in two days a week. Bunny went upstairs for a lie-down and Barbara, as if only waiting for the coast to clear, immediately appeared and, in a bid to take control of the situation, declared that the corpse had to be disposed of as soon as possible, as it was a danger to health. Sick of corpses, I replied firmly that the disposal was a matter for Bunny to decide, but Barbara retorted in turn that if there was to be a delay it was imperative to keep the corpse cool in the meantime. Thereupon she marched into the kitchen, picked up a refuse sack, took it into the utility-room, emerged a minute later with Jeeves in the sack and strode back into the kitchen, presumably on the way to carrying her package through the back door to some makeshift mortuary in an outbuilding.

A couple of hours later Bunny came down. She had regained her composure but looked pale and, despite her podginess, drawn. Jeeves's death must have been the last straw after what she has recently been through – for one can assume that Roland has confronted her on the topic of Howard. It's hard to tell from their interactions in public, for they were distant enough with each other before; but since the day Roland learnt the truth I have heard raised voices from their room and once, when we were going in to supper, I heard him hiss in Bunny's ear, 'If they only knew how much I *hate* you.' Moreover knowledge or suspicion of the scandal seems to have spread, for Barbara, in conversation over the supper in question, made some remark about 'vicious' women who had affairs with their husbands' friends. It is possible that this was a coincidence, but it's more likely that she had overheard something, as she is fond of doing. I would not put it past Howard to have confessed to her.

As we hung around the drawing-room waiting for lunch, and Amelia clucked around Bunny and plied her with more sweet tea, I asked Bunny what she wanted to do with Jeeves's remains: did she want to take them to the vet for a post-mortem? No, said Bunny, what was the point? She'd just like Jeeves to be buried in the garden. There were groans all round. Amelia's clucking ceased, her face hardened and she was just starting to say, absurdly, 'I don't think there's room in the garden,' when there was a cry from the kitchen, followed by the sound of hasty footsteps coming from there towards the drawing-room. Segunda appeared at the door. Folding her arms and setting her legs wide apart, she shouted, 'You try escare me to death. I go for guisantes in refrigerador an find Jif in Jiffy bag. Is too much. This time is too much!'

'What!' cried Bunny. 'What have you done to Jeeves?'

All eyes turned to Barbara, who assumed a look of self-righteous defiance. Bunny jumped up, shoved past Segunda – who was framed in the doorway – and hurried towards the kitchen. Segunda then theatrically turned her back on us, rapidly crossed the hall and went out through the front door, which she slammed.

Straight after the slam we heard another cry from the kitchen, this time in Bunny's voice. 'You've put him in the freezer! How *could* you!'

'I'll go and calm her down and try to rescue the lunch,' said Amelia. 'God's teeth.'

As part of the calming process, Amelia conceded that Jeeves could be buried in the garden. Sarah had contrived the discreet removal of Bernard's body, so the pets' cemetery contained a vacant and recently turned-over plot, ample for the new corpse; but Amelia, refusing to allow Jeeves into the august company of Hamish and co., designated a less dignified resting place near the vegetables. There was now the question who would dig the grave, for Mr Shanks was on holiday in Yarmouth. (Amelia had misheard Yarmouth as the Bahamas – implausible, given his likely wages from her.) Everyone but Howard and me seemed to regard the answer as obvious, and the two of us succumbed to a volley of hyperbolic tributes to our relevant experience.

The digging (relatively a piece of cake) completed, we went indoors to announce that the funeral could commence. Jeeves, having been extracted from the freezer, had been moved to the woodshed, and Bunny asked me if I would carry him from there to his final resting-place. Despite, or perhaps because of, my recent experience of far worse, I was squeamish about this, even though Jeeves was still in the sack, and I blenched to find that he was stiff – possibly from rigor mortis, possibly from his stay in the freezer, possibly a bit of each. The cortège comprised Bunny, me, Howard, Amelia and Dennis: Joy was still at the day centre (she is returned in a bus shortly before suppertime); Roland, having declined to take any interest in Jeeves's death or its sequelae, had gone for a walk (he has been doing a lot of this since his discovery of Bunny's relationship with Howard); and Barbara, although she was thick-skinned enough to start putting on her wellingtons in order to join the party, was told by Bunny to her face that her presence would be unwelcome.

After these exertions, I could have done without an unexpected pair of visitors for the supper that it was my turn to prepare. The chicken casserole would stretch only if some of us had one rather than two pieces of chicken: when I served, I made sure that I was not among the unlucky ones. It was obscure who had invited these people (Amelia, I assumed), whether they were husband and wife, or even whether there was any domestic bond between them. They were called Jack and Margery, were our sort of age and were pleasant enough – they said kind things about the death of Jeeves – but both seemed rather gaga: Jack kept repeating himself and Margery for the most part sat quietly with a chimpanzee's grin on her face.

As we were clearing away, there was a ring at the front door (the chimes have gone wrong: instead of ding-dong there's just a dong preceded by a buzz), which Amelia went to answer. On the step was a swarthy and agitated-looking man, with a Mr Whippy coiffure, accompanied by the baby policeman who had intervened in the incident at the village pond 14 hours earlier (a gruelling working day for one so young). The horrible thought occurred to me that the swarthy man might be Arnoldo & Miccolucci's Sicilian, who had come to terrorise us and been apprehended in the nick of time. Howard was more alarmed at the sight of the constable: presumably he feared that unpleasant legal consequences of his dip were starting to unfurl. 'Say I'm not here,' he whispered to the rest of us, and lumbered out of the back door in the direction of the nearest outbuilding, which was Oik's shed. An icy blast, of which I became aware after a minute, indicated that he had as usual left the back door open, so I went to shut it as Amelia led the two latest arrivals into the kitchen. The swarthy man smiled at Joy, who responded with a blank stare, but Dennis seemed to half-recognise him.

'This is PC Wiggins,' announced Amelia, 'and this is Mr Venables.' ('Venables' didn't sound Sicilian, but was it his real name?) 'Mr Venables drives the bus that delivers people home from the day centre. He has lost two of his charges and thinks they may have got off here with Joy when he wasn't looking.'

'They're called Jack and Margery,' said Venables, provoking cries of 'ha' and the like. His accent sounded English enough.

We all looked round but Jack and Margery were not to be seen: they must have wandered out of the back door which Howard had left open. A search party was formed and we broke into as many groups as there were torches. I joined PC Wiggins (a bad choice, as the radio he was wearing kept startling me with crackly bursts). Despite my efforts to deflect him, he made towards Oik's shed. When he opened the door, we found Howard squashed inside with Oik, who had presumably also gone into hiding when he had seen the police car on the drive. As we had recognised when discussing the blackmail threat, Oik doubtless has many reasons to avoid the Filth. He sprang past us and made off into the dark at a pace just short of a run, while Howard started burbling.

'Aha, constable. What a nice surprise, er, how good to see you again. Erm, I wasn't up to anything, ah, you know, with that young man. Just because I was naked on the green – ahm, we were, ah, looking for some mouse poison, no, matches.'

PC Wiggins shook his head pityingly and resumed the search for Jack and Margery, whom he ran to ground by Jeeves's new grave.

'Dennis and me,' I said to Howard as we walked back into the house, 'Amelia and Barbara, and now you and Oik. It's a queers' paradise.'

Chapter 26

•

This morning Roland came up to my room again to announce that he is moving out. He needs, he said, time and space to think. He has explained the situation to Dennis, who is going to let him use the Barbican flat for the time being.

'I'm surprised Dennis is abetting this move,' I said.

'Abetting? You make it sound as if *I'm* the wrongdoer.'

'I think you're wrong to move out. Is this temporary or permanent?'

'I don't know. As I say, I need to think things over.'

'What's Bunny meant to do?'

'That's not my main concern. She can stay here if she wants.'

'And what's she supposed to say when people ask why you have cleared off?'

'She can say what she likes. I'm writing a book in London and need to be there for research, or something.'

'The book with Peggy?' We exchanged acidic smiles. 'Have you discussed this with Bunny?'

'I've told her I'm going.'

'And what did she say?'

'She asked me not to.' I suspected that this was an understatement.

'If you want to salvage this situation –'

'What is there to salvage? The marriage has been a shell for decades.'

'In that case, why are you so upset by what's happened? If you're not around, Howard has carte blanche.'

'If she prefers Howard to me, there's nothing I can do about it.'

'That's crap. You could try being kind to her. If you'd been kinder to her in the first place, this might never have happened.'

'Fuck off. I don't need a lecture from a sexless drip like you. What do you know about the emotions? Your prick's probably withered away from lack of use.'

'Not all emotions spring from the prick.'

'You've lived your whole life without engaging with anyone. It's easy enough to carp from the sidelines.'

'Like a literary critic, you mean?'

'That's a cheap remark.'

'I wouldn't pay much more for yours.'

'If you don't commit, you can't get hurt – a convenient strategy.'

'You sound like Amelia's Psychology and Therapy manual. As to commitment, I didn't see much sign of it in your string of affairs. Your relation to Bunny has never displayed it to a high degree: you've treated her as a scullery maid.' I was quoting the phrase Bunny had used when I was eavesdropping on her and Howard. 'Perhaps if you had shown more commitment to her, she wouldn't have strayed, in which case you wouldn't have got hurt. So, contrary to what you say, failure to commit can lead to pain, just as commitment does.' I was rather pleased with this.

Roland wasn't. 'I'm not interested in that sort of clever talk,' he said.

'Not if it comes from someone other than you.'

But he didn't have the stomach for sparring. He was silent, hunched on the chair like a marabout stork.

I let up on the home truths and turned to practical consequences. 'If you move out, Bunny will too, sooner or later.'

'She said she might go to her sister's.'

'That will weaken the rest of us. Barbara will try to lever us out.'

'I don't see why.'

'Barbara —'

'The commune's had its day in any case.'

'The commune's our family, for practical purposes. And we've worked so hard to keep it going: all that business of hiding Bernard. We don't want to end up like the Soviet Union – resolutely resisting external threats and then collapsing from within.'

But Roland, in no mood for geopolitical analogies, would not be persuaded even to delay his decision. He is moving out next week.

Chapter 27

•

'It's amazing the stuff Oik has in his shed,' Howard observed over lunch, referring to his visit there when PC Wiggins had paid a call. 'It's only a piddling little place, but he's got at least 10 amplifiers stashed away, all the same make: I wish he'd lend one to me – my old thing's on the blink.' I, who was enjoying the blink, did not share this wish. 'There's also a lot of funny cellophane packets of washing powder or something. He must have a little whole-sale business we never knew about. I suppose we should take our hats off to him for enterprise.'

'You must have just climbed down from the top of the Christmas tree,' said Roland. 'The amps are stolen goods, you oaf, and the washing powder is coke.'

'Don't be silly,' Amelia said. 'Coke is black and lumpy, and they don't keep it in seelophane.'

Roland ignored this endearing display of naïveté. 'You must have seen it, Dennis? You're the only one of us to have been in there before Howard.'

Dennis looked uncomfortable and concentrated on penetrating the leathery liver that Segunda had cooked for lunch: it was not easy, with his arthritic wrists. Of the rest of us, some were trying to saw through the lumps of meat; others had foolishly put the stuff into their mouths and were masticating doggedly in the hope of reducing it to swallowable size. Amelia had largely given up, spitting out most of her half-chewed pieces and arranging them around the edge of her plate, like the stars on the European Union's flag. Howard was having trouble with his false teeth: first he thrust them forward with his tongue, so that they shot out between his lips in a macabre grin (I thought of the eroded mouth of Bernard gaping from the side of the compost heap); then he pulled out the upper set with his hand and used his thumbnail to try to extract a stringy piece of fat from between two incisors. This did nothing to rekindle our appetites, which had been extinguished by the very smell of the lunch before we had entered the dining-room.

'That's the trump card, isn't it?' chirped Bunny, who received puzzled looks in return. She smiled brightly around the table. 'It's how we frighten Oik off from blackmailing us. We tell him we know all about it.'

Pennies dropped and we lay down our knives and forks. I couldn't decide which was the greater source of relief: the prospect of thwarting Oik or the excuse to stop wrestling with the liver.

'I've never seen anything in Oik's shed,' said Dennis, guardedly, probably mendaciously, and clearly not strictly truly. After his various snipings at my lack of integrity, I thought of making something of this, but I let it go. 'Howard may have made a mistake,' he went on. 'He was in a fluster at the time.'

'Look here, I may be a bit deaf, but I've got the eyes of a hawk.'

'You've got the eyes of a whale. Anyway, hawks don't see well at close range and at night. It was dark when you went to hide in the shed. And even if you saw what you think you saw, we have no right to leap to the conclusion that Oik possesses it illegally. Maybe he does have a little business.'

This charitable conjecture provoked a chorus of derision. 'What about the powder in the plastic bags? said Roland. 'People go to gaol for running that sort of business.'

'Don't be so bloody wet, Dennis,' said Barbara, drawing on her reserves of resentment towards him. 'Do you want to carry on forking out £500 a week? We've got him by the pubes.'

Amelia gave her a Lady Bracknell look.

It all seemed too easy to me. 'Suppose we do threaten to tell the police. Oik will just get rid of the goods: then we'll be back where we were before.'

'We tell him we took a photo,' said Bunny. She was unusually on the ball today. Perhaps this was an effect of Roland's announcing his departure: I had assumed it would shatter her, but it seemed to have given her a new lease of life.

Dennis reluctantly came round and said he would have a quiet word with Oik, but Barbara wanted blood: 'Oh no you don't,' she said. 'That scum has made life a misery for all of us. He must damn well face the Inquisition. Let's get him in here right now. I saw him out the back with his motorbike.'

'I hardly think a show trial —'

Roland took Barbara's side: 'We're more intimidating en masse.'

I doubted that Oik would be greatly intimidated by a mass composed of eight crumblies, with a combined age of over 600, lolling round a lunch table, but I joined the vote in favour of Barbara's motion, which was carried by six to two – Dennis dissenting and Joy paying no attention. The next question was who should be the spokesperson. We started running through the candidates: Dennis would be too soft; Roland could be eloquent, but his rhetoric would fly over the accused's head; I was rejected for being too dry – which I decided to find flattering. Amelia cut the process short by announcing that, since she owned the house, she would do the talking. Given her tendency to lose her thread, the proposal made me nervous, and I toyed with pointing out that actually she didn't own the house: if she had owned it, we would never have needed to hide Bernard or, in consequence, got into this mess with Oik. But I let it pass: after all, we had trusted Amelia to feed alibis to Sarah, whose intellect was a lot keener than Oik's. If Amelia started to drift, the rest of us could come to the rescue. She rang her little bell for Segunda, who came in from the kitchen looking miffed: Segunda rightly views the bell as demeaning and likes to choose her own moments of entrance.

'Segunda, would you be a dear and fetch Oik – ahm – your boyfriend. We'd like a little word with him.'

Segunda's expression turned from offended to incredulous. She returned a couple of minutes later with Oik, who was greasy, having just finished overhauling his bike. Possibly for that reason, possibly to make him as uncomfortable as possible, Amelia did not offer him a seat, so he stood at the bottom end of the table, avoiding our eyes and shifting from foot to foot.

Amelia addressed him from the top end. 'We have invited you in to discuss your attempt at blackmail. Despite the hospitality you receive at The Graylings, you have seen fit to threaten me and my friends.' ('Seen fit' she got from Barbara.) 'Well, now the worm has turned. People in glass houses shouldn't throw stones. Pots shouldn't call kettles black.' Oik's brow wrinkled in the rain of proverbs, and I was wondering whether to take over already, but Amelia now bore down on her prey. 'We know that the shed which I have kindly allowed you to use contains stolen goods and illegal drugs. We also know that, if the police found out about them, you would go to prison for a long time. You have an impressive criminal record, if impressive is the word. I hope I make myself clear. You won't be getting any more payments from us. In fact, you will immediately repay to Mr Middleton the £500 you have already received from him.'

This was good stuff: terse and hard-hitting, worthy of her daughter, or of a top QC. Amelia too was on fine form today. I particularly liked the bit about repaying the £500, which I would not have thought of. She gazed sublimely down the table at Oik, like Catherine the Great in council. The other council members treated him to similar gazes. There was a silence. Oik, whose face had screwed into the sulking pout of a three-year-old, wiped his oily hands on the upholstery of the empty chair in front of him. Then he started to mumble self-contradictions at the floor.

'I dunno what you're on about. There's nothing in my shed. The stuff in there is clean. Any road, I'm clearing out the dirty stuff this afternoon.'

He spoke too quietly for Amelia to hear, so Barbara took over in a tone less dignified. 'In that case we'll phone the police this minute, you little creep. Getting rid of it won't do any good: we've got a photo. We also know about the HP Sauce.'

The mention of the HP caused Oik to superimpose a look of bafflement on his pout. Then we heard the trembling but clear voice of Segunda who, unnoticed by us, had stayed in the room and witnessed everything. 'You clear out the dirty stuff. You dirty stuff. You clear out. I have enough. You make me sick. We all sick. You clear out, dirty stuff!'

She started to cry. Howard, always ready with an arm to encircle a woman in distress, supplied one. The rest of us chimed in with 'Bravo Segunda', 'He's not good enough for you, dear' and 'Give it to him straight'. Joy started warbling 'I'm gonna wash that man right out of my hair'.

Oik banged his fist down on the table, causing one of the chewed pieces of liver that Amelia had deposited on the side of her plate to leap on to her lap. Without uttering another word, he stormed from the room, and a few seconds later we heard the roar of his bike. 'I'll getcha, you fucking cunts,' he screamed as he tore down the drive.

Chapter 28

•

I had feared that Roland's imminent exit would cast a pall over the celebrations of Joy's 80th birthday, which was today, but these went ahead as planned, starting with a special lunch. Howard, to launch the merriment, had put out some plastic peanuts to trick us during our preprandial sherry.

'Ah, lovely nuts,' Barbara said when she saw them.

'Thank you,' said Howard, looking at his crotch. He looked up for guffaws, or at least amused grins, but found neither.

There were, however, some splutters as the unsuspecting put the nuts into their mouths (Joy managed to swallow three before they were put out of her reach), but the joke went sour when Amelia damaged her dentures and had to hurry upstairs for her spare set. When she returned, she looked like Bugs Bunny.

Joy was uncertain who everyone was, so Dennis pointed to us in turn and said, 'That's Amelia [easy for anyone to mistake, as just explained], that's Barbara,' and so on.

'How clever of you to remember all those names,' said Joy in the tone of politeness that one uses to address a new acquaintance. I hoped that Barbara wouldn't maliciously ask Joy her own name, as she had done on the landing.

At the end of lunch Bunny produced a birthday cake that she had made: it was meant to be in the shape of a piano, but looked more like a surgical boot for a club-foot. There were eight candles, standing at dangerously rakish angles in sticks that were too big for them. As she brought the cake in, we all sang 'Happy Birthday' except for Roland, who remarked that we should instead be singing the 'Ode to Joy'. Although his Parkinson's was bad, he was chirpier than I have seen him since the Bunny/Howard story broke: demob-happy, perhaps. Bunny too was in high spirits. Poor Joy, however, looked miserably bewildered: despite constant reminders that this was her 80th birthday, the fact kept passing from her mind.

'Come on, darling, blow out your candles,' said Dennis.

'You never said it was *my* birthday,' Joy replied irritably.

But she gave a good blow, which extinguished three of the candles and knocked over the other five. These we hurried to put out before they could ignite the napkins – which had a holly pattern, being left over from Christmas. Amelia has insisted on using them up.

We moved into the drawing-room for coffee and charades – a popular game at The Graylings, despite our mixed abilities. Howard, the least gifted, went first. True to form, he stood in the middle of the room, looking helpless.

'Get on with it,' barked Barbara.

'I've started.'

'Do something, then.'

Howard continued to stand there like a menhir. 'Go on, guess!' he begged.

'*Moby Dick*,' proposed Dennis, causing a ripple of unkind laughter.

The answer turned out to be *Gone With the Wind* – surely easy for the flatulent Howard to have represented.

Roland, now shaking badly, went next. 'A jelly – no, a shaking – a milk-shake – Ralph Richardson,' Barbara despicably proposed. 'Am I warm?'

The answer, which we couldn't guess, was 'Nil invitus facit sapiens'. We all protested that Latin wasn't allowed. Some of us – well, I – pretend to be conversant with that language, but apart from Roland none of us understands a word.

Dennis's charade – *Hiawatha* – went wrong when he crouched down in Red Indian fashion, got trapped in that position by his arthritis and had to be rescued by Barbara and me. He was clearly in great pain. The biggest success was the charade performed by Joy, who had passed into an alert phase: unfurling herself like a flower, she did a one-movement portrayal of *Coming of Age in Samoa*. There was a touch of Margot Fonteyn about the performance.

As it was a sunny day, although cold, I suggested that we go into the garden for a round or two of Grandmother's Footsteps, my favourite party game.

'I don't think Mr Shanks will be too pleased if we walk on the lawn when it's frosty,' said Amelia in her saccharine manner.

'Bugger Mr Shanks,' said Joy, and as it was her party she carried the day.

Amelia was appointed the first grandmother, and she irritated her stalkers by turning round too often: none of us could get more than a couple of steps from base, so we replaced her with Dennis, who marked his status by inserting a set of funny teeth. Howard, trying to be clever and spring on Dennis from the side, started a detour through a flower bed, but his gaff was blown by Amelia who, invoking Mr Shanks's dim views, protested at the damage to the plants. The round came to an end when Joy started walking off at a right angle and Dennis had to chase after her as if she were a two-year-old. As he retrieved her from the rough, she turned nasty and slapped him hard in the face, knocking off his glasses.

Dennis bravely laughed this off as he retrieved them. 'Come on, old girl, time for a cup of tea, I think.'

Chapter 29

•

The birthday party had an invigorating effect on our esprit de corps: Amelia should report this to her fellow students on the team-building project. Over breakfast the next morning we savoured the high points of the day. Howard remarked that the funny teeth which Dennis had inserted were so like Dennis's own that no-one had noticed them till they were pointed out. Dennis opened his mouth to deliver a counter-quip, but no sound came out. Assuming that something had lodged in his throat, Barbara leapt up and thumped him on the back. But Dennis wasn't choking or unable to breathe: he just couldn't speak. He looked perplexedly around, opening and shutting his mouth like an expiring fish, while the rest of us exchanged worried glances. Barbara declared that Dr Pee should be called, and she thudded out to the phone. Pee arrived, carried out a brief examination and diagnosed a minor stroke: Dennis, he said, should be driven immediately to hospital for a brain scan. Bunny tactlessly asked whether and when Dennis would be able to speak again, but Pee brushed the question aside, saying that he had to get on with arranging the scan.

Barbara drove Dennis to the hospital and Bunny went too. At lunchtime Bunny phoned to say that Dennis, while waiting for the scan, had had another stroke, which had deprived him of sensation and movement down one side. He was therefore being admitted as an in-patient. Bunny promised to phone later with more news. We meanwhile had the job of keeping Joy on an even keel: she was aware that something worrying had happened involving Dennis, but was unclear what it was. 'Dennis is late,' she repeated fretfully. We tried to distract her with the jigsaw of the firemen, then with the piano, then with the prospect of an afternoon nap, but were running out of ideas: Dennis was so much more experienced at this than we. At seven in the evening Bunny phoned again to say that Dennis had suffered a third stroke, which had killed him.

Dennis was one of my dearest friends, but I was not shaken by the news. Perhaps I am a cold fish: Roland may have been right that I know little of the emotions, but the upside of a life of detachment is that losses are easy to bear. Or perhaps it's old age: you resign yourself to the fact that you and your friends are all dry brown leaves who must soon be blown off the tree.

When Bunny and Barbara returned home it was agreed that for the moment we would lie to Joy that Dennis had been kept in hospital for some tests. Bunny heroically agreed, after her taxing day, to put Joy to bed, while Barbara – stirred by the opportunity for action and bossiness – got on the phone to notify the Middleton children. It turned out that their daughter Gillian was the only one of them in England, so it fell to her to decide what sort of funeral to have and what to do with Joy. As to the former, Gillian's decision was guided by principles that she labelled 'natural death' and 'humanism': together these apparently entailed that Dennis should be buried, without intervention of undertakers, clergy or civic officials, in a garden or field.

'Before you even suggest it,' said Amelia, 'he's not going in my garden.'

Jeeves had clearly been the line in the sand. It proved too hard to find a suitable plot in the time available, which was short, for the hospital's mortuary was overflowing – a poor advertisement for the service provided in the wards – and its supervisor wanted Dennis out to make room for new arrivals. Gillian therefore settled for cremation, but still insisted on dispensing with undertakers and their paraphernalia. She herself drove Dennis to the crematorium: he was lying not in a coffin but in a giant wicker Moses basket and was covered by a sheet, which Gillian insisted on pulling back for us to say our farewells. Dennis's mouth was stretched in a ghastly grin, and the sight of his crooked yellow teeth reminded me momentarily of our game of Grandmother's Footsteps.

The events at the crematorium were ugly. There was a conveyor-belt of mourners: when we arrived, we had to queue behind the party in front, who had not yet gone in, and when we came out we had to elbow our way past the next lot, who were already pushing their way inside. In the crush it was hard to tell which flowers went with which cremation: Amelia was appalled to think that the wreath of daisies that spelled BYE BYE NAN might be associated with us. The proceedings were conducted by an official from the Humanist Association, a hard-faced woman in late middle age who, save for her blue rinse, looked and dressed like a warder from Holloway. She told us that, for humanists, immortality consists of being remembered by your friends.

'Immortality Lite,' Roland whispered to me. 'If I'd

known that that was what it was, I'd have been nicer to my friends.'

Howard then went forward to read Dennis's favourite poem, 'The Darkling Thrush'. It is an affecting piece at any time, and in these circumstances it was too much for Howard, who started to weep and was unable to complete the reading. After that disgusting display, a small pair of doors opened behind the Moses basket, which was on a platform, and there was a whirring noise that reminded me of the Escalope: the basket was resting on rollers, and the whirring came from these as they started to propel Dennis through the doors and into the furnace. It was hard not to giggle. Once the basket had disappeared, the little doors closed with an undignified slam.

Throughout the service Joy was confused and restless. 'Dennis is late,' she kept saying. 'Where's Dennis?' By now she had been told that he was dead, but the information wouldn't sink in, so we had to keep telling her again. Each time she was reminded, it seemed to her as if she were learning the news for the first time, which of course produced a paroxysm of shock and grief. It was like a torture from Dante.

Amelia, possibly embarrassed by the hard line she had taken on the question of burial, agreed that a tree in memory of Dennis could be planted in the garden; she also agreed, distinguishing between ashes and a body in its unreduced state, that Dennis's ashes could first be sprinkled into the hole for the tree. Once they had cooled down, a couple of days after the funeral, Gillian and I drove back to the crematorium and were given some ashes that the superintendent told us were Dennis's. Gillian doesn't believe in urns, so she scooped the ashes into a cylindrical biscuit tin without a lid. Perhaps because she is a votary of the 'natural', perhaps because she wanted to dispel any remaining whiff of corpse, she insisted on having the window of the car wide open, despite the raw weather: as we picked up speed, the ashes started blowing out of the tin, into our faces and through the window. I warned her that at this rate there would be nothing left of Dennis by the time we got home.

Mr Shanks had got the hole ready for the planting ceremony. It was in the middle of a cluster of saplings which Amelia altruistically intends will grow into a small wood in a couple of decades. The memorial plaque was not yet ready, so, once Dennis's sapling was in, we attached to it a temporary label that just said 'Dennis'. During the gale that blew the following night, the label came off, and there is now a debate as to which of the saplings is the commemorative one.

Chapter 30

•

Joy has been moved to a nearby home called Atkins House. The day after Gillian had settled her in, Bunny, Howard and I took a taxi and went to visit. The building, an attractive white one in the style of Lutyens, is set in grounds, and as we were about to drive through the gate an elderly and of-ficial-looking man stepped in front of the taxi and held up his hand. Our driver opened the side window and the man bent down to look through.

'We've come to visit one of the residents,' Bunny leant forward to say. 'Do we just carry on up the drive?'

The man's jaw slowly dropped as he continued to stare through the window without replying; then he started to grin. We should have twigged to his being one of the in-mates from the fact that he had kept his hand raised while bending down by the car.

When we entered the building I noticed first the smell of lavender air freshener and then, under it, that of old pee. The receptionist told us that Joy had been put on the top floor: there were three storeys, she said, and the higher the one you were on, the higher the level of care you were con-sidered to need, so Joy was getting the full service. We were greeted at the top by a black man wearing a plastic overall and rubber gloves, who cheerily informed us that we would find Joy in the day-room at the end of the corridor. As we walked down it, we saw strange scenes through the door-ways of the bedrooms: there was a man (I think it was a man) sitting on his bed with a blanket over his head; another one was standing mumbling to himself, shuffling his feet and rolling his fingers and thumbs as if making bread pellets; then a tiny and distraught lady darted out of her room, seized me by the arm and gazed at me beseechingly.

'Doctor,' she said in a voice like crow's, 'is this the end?'

'It feels like it,' I replied as I pulled myself free.

The day-room provided a spectacle of the last stages of physical and mental decay. One of the specimens was burbling gibberish, another was going ba-ba-ba, a third – past being able to sit up – was lying in a sort of pram and dribbling on to a pillow. The phrase 'second childhood' didn't do justice to them: this was second early babyhood. Joy was sitting in the corner watching, or at any rate facing, the telly, which had a game show on. Her hair, which for the past 50 years had been elegantly drawn back to a bun, was a chaotic frizz: it had been washed, but no-one had bothered even to comb it. She looked like an angelic scarecrow. Joy showed no sign of pleasure, or even interest, on seeing us. When we had drawn three chairs into a semicircle round her (they had non-absorbent covers), Bunny asked her how she liked Atkins House.

'Dennis is meant to be picking me up,' Joy replied. 'He's late. Where is he?'

'You know about Dennis, darling: we told you,' Bunny said gently. 'He died. We're all very sad.'

'Thank heaven,' Joy replied briskly. 'I thought he was *late*.'

Howard went to look for a lav, and as soon as he had gone a burly old man came and loomed over my chair, bringing his face within three inches of mine. 'Father!' he exclaimed in an awe-struck voice. It wasn't clear whether he thought I was his father or a priest.

'Hallo,' I said as coolly as I could while trying to move my face away. 'What's your name?'

'Dennis!' he shouted, giving me a start.

I foresaw confusion arising from this. The new Dennis held out his hand for me to shake, and when I did so my hand slid up to his wrist, for he was lacking a thumb. Then he plonked himself down in Howard's seat and stared catatonically ahead while Bunny and I tried to continue our already faltering conversation with Joy.

From across the room we heard, 'I'm havin' a wee! I'm havin' it now!' The cry came from a toothless man who was being visited by his family.

'It's all right, Dad, you've got your bag,' his embarrassed son (there was a strong resemblance) said as quietly as he could, but this failed to placate the old boy, who shouted, 'I wanna go for a walk! I'm havin' a wee!'

The son got him to his feet and walked him out of the room, presumably while he was still weeing. I thought it was only rats that urinated on the go.

Then the cheery black man who had been, but was no longer, wearing the overall and rubber gloves appeared at the door and called, 'Teatime, everybody.' I was thinking that a piece of Victoria sponge would go down a treat, but, judging by the nauseating smell of institutional mince that was now wafting in from the corridor, tea was high tea, even though it was only five o'clock. Various other black people appeared to usher or push the inmates to the dining-room, and one attendant started chivvying Bunny,

Howard and me along with the rest. One might, I suppose, mistake Howard for an old wreck needing 24-hour nursing, but Bunny and I were, as we both thought, well turned out and obviously in possession of our faculties.

In the dining-room the smell of mince was strong enough to make you gag, and the three of us made eye contact to the effect of 'Let's go'.

'We'll just see you to your table, darling,' Bunny said to Joy, 'then we'll be on our way.'

Joy wasn't paying attention. 'Someone's in my place!' she cried. 'Nurse, tell her she can't sit there!'

The usurper was the tiny crow-voiced lady who had asked me whether this was the end, but the attendant had a more pressing matter to deal with by the door: it appeared that Dennis could perceive in the dining-room something even worse than the mince, the watery greens, the lumpy mash and the drooling diners, for he had wedged himself in the doorway and was crying, 'I'm not going in, I'm not going in!' It took three attendants – two pushing and one pulling – to get him into the room. Once this had been accomplished, one of them returned to sort out the dispute between Joy and the crow lady.

'I can't see what the fuss is about,' Howard murmured to me. 'Wherever you sit, you've got to eat a plate of dog's vomit and talk to a lot of crackpots.'

I reminded him that routine is comforting. The attendant coaxed the crow into vacating Joy's seat and roosting on an empty perch at the next table. Once Joy was settled, we each gave her a kiss.

'See you soon, Joy,' said Howard.

'Lots of love,' said Bunny.

Joy barely glanced at us: she had started pushing her fork around in the puddle of mince on her plate. We walked across the room, past the man with the blanket over his head. He kept it on while eating, lifting the front slightly to get the food underneath.

'We can't leave her in that zoo,' Bunny said as we went down in the lift. 'She may be a bit dotty, but she deserves better than that, poor old thing.'

We asked to see the manager and urged her to move Joy to one of the other floors. The manager, who was sympathetic, explained that there were currently no spaces available but said that she would see what she could do at the end of the month, when one resident was due to move out from the first and one from the ground floor. Bunny asked if we could have a look at those floors, and we were given a tour. There was much less of the chamber of horrors about them, and the ground floor was particularly attractive: each room gave out on to a terrace, from which you could walk down into the grounds, and the residents seemed sane and fit enough. Joy, the manager said, probably wouldn't be suited to this floor, but she might be all right on the first.

'That's where they're Upton Park, then,' said Howard. The manager looked at him inquiringly. 'Two stops short of Barking,' Howard explained with a chortle, and received a chilly smile.

'It's Becontree,' I said to him as we left the building.
'Eh?'
'The expression: two stations *beyond* Barking.'

'It's two coupons short of a pop-up toaster, so it should be short of Barking.'

'Becontree *is* short of Barking if you approach it from Upminster.'

'You'd be barking to go to Upminster in the first place.'

Chapter 31

•

It's an old saw that time passes more quickly the older you get: someone said that one of the pleasures of old age is that breakfast seems to come round every quarter of an hour. The pleasures perhaps only seem more frequent, but among the old the horrors really do occur more often. Less than a month after Dennis's death, Fate dealt The Graylings another hammer blow. I was woken one morning by an urgent tapping on my door and by Barbara's voice calling my name. From her tone it was clear, even through the door and my hypnopompic fog, that she was in a state. There was none of the usual hectoring stridency: it was the voice of a woman terrified. I got out of bed, shuffled to the door, opened it and found Barbara in her dormitory-issue flannel pyjamas. I gave her an inquiring and unfriendly look. The look I received was directed not at my face but over my shoulder.

'Is that you?' Barbara said. 'I can't see. I can't see!' She was breathing rapidly and trembling.

'What do you mean?' I said testily.

'I'm blind. I've woken up blind.' She reached out and grabbed my arms.

It was true. Barbara has since 'seen' a specialist, who has started a course of treatment but has been noticeably silent on the probability of her regaining her sight. I have had to resist the temptation to hide her things, to leave obstacles in her path, and to do away with Moth (perhaps strangling him in front of her, without her realising) or at least to shut him away. But there is no need to intervene to make Barbara miserable, for she is profoundly miserable already. Given her energy, she will likely adjust to her condition and rally in due course, but at present her spirit is broken and she spends most of the day in her room listening to the radio: what else can she do to pass the time?

It is little comfort to the rest of us that, if Barbara was planning to bring down the commune, she has been handicapped in her efforts, for the commune is collapsing of its own accord. Dennis is, in Segunda's phrase, dead as a yo-yo, Joy has been deported to Atkins and Roland has moved out, which leaves Amelia, Barbara, Bunny, Howard and me. We all recognise that this is not a viable social unit and, when we gathered for our management meeting today, it was clear – even though there was no printed agenda, for Barbara never learnt to touch-type – that we were going to have to discuss the process for bringing our arrangement to a dignified end. I was taken aback to discover that the others have all made plans that are well advanced. Bunny, as Roland indicated, is going to stay with her sister. I speculated on the possibility that Bunny and Roland would get together again: the stay with the sister is presumably meant to be temporary and, now Dennis is dead, Roland's tenure in the Barbican is insecure. Then I reflected that here was an opportunity for Bunny and Howard to live together at last; but that is unlikely, for Howard announced that Peggy has offered to put him up while he looks for somewhere else. This game to Howard, then, in the match with Roland – if the match is still on. The blind Barbara will stay on with the deaf Amelia; so Barbara has at last got what she seemed to want, but not on the terms she had hoped for or expected.

'And what are *your* plans, dear?' Amelia asked me, in a tone so sweet that it could only mean: 'You'd better pack your bags, moosh, and sod off.'

I don't have any plans. I asked for time to think.

Chapter 32

•

I have bagged the newly vacant room on the ground floor
of Atkins House. The arrangement isn't perfect – the tellies
of the other residents are a trial and the food wins no
rosettes (it's better than the muck they serve to the ancient
babies on the top floor and, for that matter, than Segunda's
liver or Roland's Gammon Delight) – but on balance I'm
content. I soon ceased to notice the smell of pee, I'm un-
obtrusively looked after, I have no responsibilities, I'm not
required to be more than distantly courteous to my neigh-
bours, and when my savings run out – as they soon will –
the taxpayer will pay for me to stay on. I come and go as I
like: so far I have been back to visit Amelia and Barbara –
both more agreeable, now that the pressure of proximity
has been removed – and have stayed the night with Peggy
and Howard after a hilarious dinner party at their house.
The two of them are developing into a possibly enduring
ménage. On fine days I go for a walk in the grounds of
Atkins House with Joy, who has been moved to the first
floor.

When I was younger I dreaded the prospect of ending up
in a home, but like many things, when it happens, it isn't
so bad.

First published in Great Britain by:

Ashgrove Publishing

an imprint of:
Hollydata Publishers Ltd
27 John Street
London WC1N 2BX

ISBN 978 185398 185 2

First Edition

Book design by Brad Thompson

Printed and bound in England